While certain historical figures and events grace the pages of this book the novel itself is entirely fictional as creative licensing has been taken in the formation of the story and the characters that are portrayed.

Kyle,

all my best!

Conor Jennings

"We'd all be speaking German, living under the flag of Japan
If it wasn't for the Good Lord and the man"
-John Rich

Southeast of Besançon, France

October 15, 1943

0130 hours

The tremors from his heartbeat rivaled only those of the San Andreas Fault as Thomas lay there under a tiny footbridge in the woods, silent as a church mouse.

Those Krauts are either deaf, blind, or just fucking stupid, he thought, knowing a few slabs of stone were all that separated him from a pair of German soldiers who wanted nothing more than to pump his bruised and battered body full of lead.

Each footstep from above raised his pulse, but after what seemed like an eternity, the Nazis crossed the bridge. Where they were going, he didn't care, but they were off the bridge, and he had *just* enough of a window to get back into the woods.

"How in holy hell did I end up here?" First Lieutenant Thomas Whitney of the U.S. Army Air Corps whispered to himself as he got up from under the bridge and quietly bolted toward a wooded area that could very well have been crawling with Germans. He didn't care, though. He knew he needed to go east toward Switzerland and obtain a one-way ticket away from this shit show. How far was the Swiss border? He had no real idea, but once again, he knew it was his only way to get out of France alive. The last time his feet were on mainland Europe was during a family trip as a teenager that saw him stare down one of Europe's other notable dictators. Now, he wouldn't be staring down a dictator as much as he'd be avoiding that dictator's ruthless soldiers.

As he traversed the woods, he made sure to be as quiet as possible. Hearing a twig crack in the darkness sent a shiver down his spine. He clearly wasn't alone. The sounds of snapping sticks and crunching leaves kept getting closer and closer, and once again, Thomas's heart beat could break the sound barrier. Finally, the noise was close enough that he could make out a shape in the pitch-black night. It wasn't really visible, but he *could* see that this was a figure much too small and under-equipped to be a German soldier. It could be a French resistance fighter or even a pro-Nazi collaborator, but the person was getting closer, and Thomas was ready for anything.

Finally, Thomas sprung out of his crouch and tackled the stranger, whom he quickly realized was a woman. He pinned her down, holding a finger to his lips, a hand over her mouth. He was aware that there could still be Germans in the area, although any enemies would have already heard the commotion and become suspicious. "Can you help me?" was all he could say softly.

The startled, frail young woman took a deep breath and collected her thoughts as Thomas gently pulled his hand off her mouth while still holding her down. "*Parlez-vous Francais*?"

Thomas had barely passed French class back at Deerfield Academy, and that was thanks to his French teacher, Mrs. Sittig, being so kind as to bump his grade up a few points. He did have the basics of the French language down pat and responded, "*Non*. Only English."

"You're lucky my mother is from London and I speak English. Otherwise, we'd have troubles," the suddenly calm woman replied as Thomas still held on to her as he suspicions had not been put to rest.

"Thomas Whitney, U.S. Army Air Corps," he said, as he let her go and extended a hand.

"Rebecca," she replied as she, too, extended a hand. "Rebecca Couture. How did you end up here?"

"My P-51 got shot down this afternoon, and I've been laying low in the woods ever since. Dodged a few German patrols. I think they're gone for now, but they'll be back. I'm trying to get to Switzerland. Can you help me?"

"I'm trying to get to the border, too. I'll lead the way and translate, if need be. You can be my protection. You have a gun, right?" Rebecca asked, feeling a mutually beneficial partnership forming before her.

"I've got my two sidearms." Thomas brandished his government-issue .45 caliber and his personal six-shooter revolver. "Here. Take this," Thomas said as he handed her his .45 to spread out the proverbial wealth of fire power. He held on to the inconsistent six-shooter that he himself had never fired, almost immediately regretting the decision. But if he and Rebecca got into a gunfight with German troops, the duo was as good as dead-it wouldn't matter who had what gun then.

"Thank you," Rebecca answered as she looked over the piece of American firepower in her hand. She had never held a gun, much less fired one in combat, but holding it made her feel empowered. For the first time since the war began, she'd be able to take revenge against the

German soldiers for what they had done to her, her family, and countless other innocents throughout Europe.

As she was analyzing her borrowed gun, Thomas asked, "Why are you going to Switzerland? Especially now? You've been occupied for three years now."

"The time was right. Let's try to be as quiet as possible. We're only fifty miles from the border, but I'm afraid there are more Germans here than in all of Munich. Things change quickly, and it's not like the rest of your American army is coming any time soon," Rebecca answered.

"I don't think the armada is coming this week," Thomas said in reference to the buildup of troops and supplies in England that were still almost a year from crossing the Channel to storm Hitler's *Fetsung Europa.*

"We have about four hours until sunrise. Let's get as far as we can tonight, and stay low during the day. Try to stay out of sight," Rebecca said.

"What do you mean?"

"I mean there are patrols everywhere, and the best way to avoid them is to move at night and take cover during the day."

"So, you're saying become nocturnal?"

"If that's what you want to call it, then fine. But let's go. We can make it to the border in forty-eight hours if we start now."

"Then what are we waiting for?" Thomas asked as the newly formed duo made their way east.

Mum was the word as both tried not to so much as crunch a leaf. Autumn was upon Europe, and the foliage that would have aided their stealth was long gone. Instead, the leaves now served as terrestrial noisemakers that could alert a suspicious member of the Wehrmacht, if one happened to be in earshot.

The two navigated the woods of southern France all night and found a rocky crevice deep in the forest to take cover in during the day.

"This isn't exactly the Ritz in New York," Thomas said as he sat down on a large boulder at the bottom of the rocky embankment.

"It's better than being in a camp, though. There's a major highway that leads directly into Bern about a mile from here. There's a lot of German tanks and trucks on it every day and foot patrols everywhere, so we need to keep a low profile. Let's take turns sleeping and make sure someone is keeping a lookout at all times. I'll be the first watch," Rebecca said as she sat down across from Thomas and rested her feet on a boulder.

Despite being exhausted, neither Thomas nor Rebecca could get to sleep. They couldn't just shut off the rush of adrenaline they both had from being on the run, and sleeping on boulders in the middle of an enemy-occupied woodland wasn't exactly conducive to beauty rest.

The awkward silence was broken when Thomas asked, "Are you with the Resistance?"

"God, no. I'm not trying to fight. I'm trying to get to my sister in Bern. She's the only family I have left. If I don't get out of here, I'm dead, too."

"What happened to your family?"

"We had been hiding out for years from the Nazis until yesterday when they found us. I escaped, but they got my parents. If they're not dead now they will be soon," Rebecca said as a tear ran down her face.

"Why was your family in hiding? Were you criminals?"

"Our only crime is being Jewish, even though we never really cared enough to seriously practice," Rebecca replied.

"So, they just round up Jews and take them away?" Thomas replied. He had never heard of anything like it before. This certainly wasn't being discussed in the news back home or in England for that matter. He wondered if the President Roosevelt and the rest of the government knew anything about it.

"Yes, that's what the Nazis do. They want to be rid of us," Rebecca confirmed.

"If the Nazis were rounding you up, then why didn't any of you fight back? This would have never happened in America," Thomas said oblivious to the rounding up of Japanese Americans that was taking place in the wake of Pearl Harbor

"Are you serious? Whatever became of your American Indians? Don't tell me America is the perfect paradise where no one gets hurt. Escape in the middle of the night knowing your family will likely never be seen or heard from again, and you might understand why we didn't do something."

"I didn't mean it like that." Thomas wanted to say more. As an American, he had every right to throw FDR and American policy under the bus, but for a foreigner to do it was unacceptable, but he bit his tongue this time around.

"Well, it came out like that. Besides, if *we* had our own fucking country, then maybe this whole nightmare could be avoided."

"Maybe," Thomas replied as he began massaging his left wrist.

Rebecca was getting sleepy-eyed and, by this point, was more than annoyed with her American "partner," but she noticed him favoring his wrist. "Are you hurt?"

"When I bailed out yesterday, I hit it," he said, pointing at the wrist with his right hand. "I aggravated an old football injury."

Looking him up and down, she asked, "Were you a goalkeeper?" Rebecca thought he was referring to soccer, but Thomas was too tired to correct her. The adrenaline was now wearing off, and due to sheer exhaustion, Thomas was now finding the rocks they were hiding among to be quite comfortable and started to doze off.

"Yes," Thomas replied. "I was the last line of defense."

Los Angeles, California

January 1, 1940

The sun had just started to go down on a beautiful New Year's evening in southern California, and it was time to kick off the Rose Bowl AKA "Granddaddy of them of all" in Pasadena. The University of Southern California Trojans were set to kick to the Tennessee Volunteers, and Thomas was on the kickoff team, looking to open his final collegiate game up with a bang. After sitting out freshman season due to rules that banned freshmen from varsity sports, he'd emerged as one of the leaders on an elite Trojans team that was among the class of college football. Thomas loved being an enforcer from the safety position, and he brought that with him to special teams.

The ball was in the air and he was charging down the field. He was a special teams gunner and that meant sacrificing one's body-something he was all for- to make a play. There was nothing Thomas loved more than laying out opposing returners with a thunderous hit and then reporting to his safety position behind the line of scrimmage to do it all over again to open a game. The Volunteers' obnoxiously fluorescent orange jerseys brought out the junkyard dog in him, as he shredded an oncoming blocker as the returner fielded the ball near the fifteen-yard line. But the returner hadn't made it to the seventeen when Thomas reached him and laid him out with a violent hit that sent him to the ground. Now, Tennessee would have lousy field position to open the game.

The Volunteer wasn't the only thing to pop on impact. Thomas's left wrist twisted in a way that human wrists aren't supposed to. A sharp, shooting pain made it seem like his left hand was hanging on by a thread—or maybe a tendon. For a brief second, he thought about sidelining himself, but he had a safety position to man.

All through the game, Thomas did everything he could to take down ball carriers without using his left hand and arm. He was in agony, but the Volunteers didn't have a clue, and couldn't use it against him. If they'd had the slightest clue that the star safety and defense leader was playing with a bum wrist, the Tennessee ball carriers would have been running circles around him like a JV/varsity scrimmage.

In the end, the Trojans took home a 14-0 win over the previously undefeated Vols. It wasn't all good news for Thomas, though, as he'd done some serious damage to his wrist. Playing through it only compounded the problem, but he wouldn't take himself out of a pickup game at the park, much less his last ever collegiate game on the biggest stage there is. Coming off the field, his parents, Matthew and Katlyn, came to meet him. A congratulatory handshake from his father made the pain in Thomas's left wrist very apparent.

"I thought I saw it on the field, and now I really notice it," his father said. "Why didn't you let someone take a look at it?" He tried to examine his son's banged up extremity.

"Didn't want to leave the game—not when it's the last one in college and there's no chance I go pro."

He respected the fight in his son, and as much as he wanted to lecture him on the importance of his health, he knew it would be falling on deaf ears. Thomas was the definition of free-spirited maverick, and when he set his mind to something, there was absolutely no talking him out of it.

"Your mother and I are staying at the Beverly Wilshire tonight, and we're not going home until tomorrow. You're more than welcome to join us if you'd like."

"No, thank you; the boys and I are going out for one last go-round—you know, raise a little hell and celebrate like only Trojans can."

"Have fun, honey, and don't stay out too late. You've got a big final semester coming up," his mother chimed in, since she'd been uncharacteristically quiet during this mini-family reunion in the bowels of the now-empty Rose Bowl.

"Get that wrist checked out. I'll give my friend Dr. Porter a call; if you'd like, he can have you good as new before too long," his father suggested.

"I'll handle it on my own," said a rebellious Thomas. "Thank you, though."

"Just think: this time next year, you'll be Mr. Whitney, English teacher to a group of lucky children," Mrs. Whitney added.

"I can't wait," Thomas said with a sense of sarcasm. His collegiate days were winding down, and his tenure as a college athlete was through. The *real* world was coming on hard, but he still had time to enjoy himself.

"Love you," his mother said. "See you soon," said his father.

"Love you, too," Thomas said as they all embraced and headed their separate ways—the elder Whitneys to a night at one of the world's most prestigious hotels, and their son to a night of celebratory debauchery.

As he walked across the field for a final time, he thought about the life he thought awaited him as an educator. It was a far cry from the glory of playing college football, but evolution was a fact of life, and Thomas would need to embrace that. Between his college football days and a certain trip to Europe in the mid-1930s he had some interesting life experiences that school children would be lucky to learn. His wrist wouldn't be a hindrance right now, because there were good times to be had tonight, and the pure joy of celebrating a much deserved victory would trump any pain he had. Short-term joy for a lengthy run of pain seemed like a deal with the devil well worth making.

***

Unknown Location Between Besançon and the Swiss Border

October 15, 1943

1030 hours

Thomas and Rebecca had taken turns watching for enemy patrols, but today, the Nazis had other priorities, so the partners never heard a footstep. What their rocky accommodations lacked in comfort, they made up for in safety—at least they were able to get *some* rest ahead of their big night traversing the French countryside. Thomas reached for the one item of food he had-a chocolate bar that by some miracle known but to God and the people at Hershey's didn't melt when he crashed. Being the chivalrous gentleman he was, he broke the bar and gave half to the nearly-asleep Rebecca.

"I never was much of a chocolate fan, but I needed this. *Merci beaucoup*," Rebecca said as she took a small bite and planned on savoring the rest.

"You're welcome. Might be the last food we have until we reach the border."

"I don't know about you, but I can go two days without eating, especially if there's freedom on the other side."

"I can, too," Thomas said, as he finished what was left of his chocolate bar.

An awkward silence followed, and Rebecca wanted to break it. Being on the run wasn't the best atmosphere for small talk, and she wasn't feeling chatty, especially after witnessing her entire family being hauled to their deaths. But if the two of them were going to help each other get to freedom, she'd have to try. "Where did you fly your plane out of?" she asked.

"England. Been stationed over there for a few months now."

"Did you like being in the U.K.?"

"It's okay; I'd rather be on a Pacific Island drinking mai-tais and slaying Nips, but it's not the worst place I've ever been," Thomas said. Being marooned on a tropical island in the

Pacific sounded much better than the reality he was living right now. At the very least, it'd be warmer.

"I only ask because I was supposed to go to Oxford before this all happened," Rebecca said as the bloodiest conflict in human history was summarized as *this*.

"Oxford? No kidding, you must be pretty smart."

"Thank you. My parents both graduated from there and met while they were attending. My mom is actually from London—that's why I can speak English."

"And I assume your father is French?"

"Yes, his father was Jewish, and his mother was Catholic. He was raised Jewish, but he never really passed it on to us."

"That's how my family was with Catholicism. We got the gist of it, went to church and did all that, but never got a whole lot out of it. I'm religious right now, though. I've prayed more in the last twenty-four hours than I did in my first twenty-five years on the planet."

"At times like these, we need something bigger than ourselves to hold on to."

"How did a pretty girl like you get so philosophical?"

"Unlike your American beauties in swimsuits, spending their entire lives at the beach, I was book smart. I was raised by a pair of educated parents who challenged me and didn't coddle me."

"Are you saying I was coddled as a child?" Thomas asked defensively.

"Please. I've known you for no more than a few hours, and your snobbery is painfully apparent."

She paused at his expression. "Maybe you're right," she replied, realizing she was making assumptions about this near-stranger. "I'm sorry for being so snappy. If we're going to get out of this alive, we need to trust each other and not get worked up over meaningless things."

"Water under the bridge," Thomas said, as he thought about the new meaning that phrase had taken over the last few hours. He realized *just* how snobby he must seem to her, and how all his material comfort went out the window when the attack on Pearl Harbor happened.

***

Santa Monica, California

December 7, 1941

Starting in the 1700s, right into the mid-20th century, the North River just south of Boston was one of the principal shipbuilding hubs of North America, as clipper after clipper came from shipyards along its banks. The Whitney family had made their fortune over several decades on one of those stretches of riverbank. Thomas's great-grandfather had founded Whitney Shipping shortly before the Civil War, and his grandfather would keep the company going strong into the 1900s. By the early 20th century, however, the landscape had changed as East Coast shipbuilding slowed down. The money was in California—San Diego, to be precise—as the Pacific was quickly becoming the new hub of shipbuilding. Clippers were becoming as synonymous with San Diego as beautiful weather and palm trees.

Thomas's father, Matthew, had inherited the family business after returning from Russia in World War I, planning to conquer the business world and the high seas. Matthew's brother, Craig, also served in the Great War, but stayed out of business and traveled around the world as a U.S. diplomat, often sailing on Whitney ships to get from A to B. Coming from such a well-off family made life very easy for Thomas and gave him opportunities that most his age could only dream of.

After failing miserably during his first year of teaching in Del Mar, outside of San Diego, Thomas moved up the coast to Santa Monica and found work in a watering hole called Junction that overlooked the Pacific. Surely, bartending with a college degree wasn't what his overly uppity parents had in mind for their only son, but it was a means to an end, and he was out of their proverbial hair. He was in so many ways a remittance man, and that didn't bother him at all. Money in the 1940s was hard to come by, and the Whitneys were one of the few families that had coin to spare, so he took it guiltlessly.

Thomas didn't know the first thing about the restaurant industry, but the owner, Patrick Hanson, was a diehard Trojans fan who was more than happy to employ a former Trojan. The way Thomas looked at it, even a capuchin monkey could operate a beer tap and/or make a gin martini. Sailors, tourists, locals, and everyone in between came to Junction for spirits, fun times, and Thomas's antics and bravado. Being a former college ball player who could work any room with his sense of humor made him a hit with everyone that came in there—especially the ladies.

The morning of December 7, 1941 was like any other Sunday morning for Thomas, as he was in bed, nursing a hangover. This Sunday was different, as he had to be in the bar an hour before noon to set up for a lunch function.

Thomas rolled over and checked his watch. "Fuck." Five after eleven—he was *already* late for work. He stormed through his apartment, threw on last night's clothes, hopped on his Harley, and flew the few miles to Junction. By the time he pulled into the empty restaurant, it was twenty past eleven—late, but salvageable. Patrick had grown used to his antics and was always willing to put up with some, because, generally, they didn't make his life harder, and Thomas's positives helped line Pat's pockets with plenty of money.

"Sorry I'm late, Mr. Hanson. I had a little too much fun last night," Thomas said as he got behind the bar to make sure there was enough ice and champagne to satisfy his thirsty guests.

"Did you hear the news?" Patrick said as he sat next to at the bar with the radio playing throughout the room.

"What news?"

"The Japs bombed Hawaii—we're at war, son."

Thomas stood there, momentarily speechless—a very rare occurrence. "They just *bombed* the islands?" he asked, trying to make sense of what was going on. America would now have to join the worldwide conflict it had been gleefully ignoring for years and Thomas knew he'd have to sign on the dotted line.

"Yup—Pearl Harbor Navy Base. I guess they hit our boys hard, and it's not over yet, not by a longshot. Get your uniform on. As of today, your bartending days are over," Patrick said echoing the sentiments of Thomas-it was time to enlist.

As the anger welled up in him, Thomas began to feel obliged to help his country avenge the sucker punch it had just taken. He may not have even liked President Roosevelt, but it looked like he'd be going to war to fight on his behalf.

"I'll go to the recruiting station first thing in the morning."

"I think the party is probably cancelled, but if you want to stick around, feel free. Would you like a cup of coffee? I just put a fresh pot on."

"Yes, please," he said. He stood pensively, then said, "I sure don't want to end up like one of our boys in Italy, stuck in the mud for months at a time like in *A Farewell to Arms*."

Patrick poured him a nice cup of black and placed it in front of him before sitting right back down. "You're a college graduate and a bit of daredevil—why not sign up to be a pilot? Don't have to sit in some jungle and get shit on by birds and eat powdered eggs."

"Who made you a recruiter?" Thomas answered with a smile as he took a sip of the piping hot coffee.

"I've been in the game for a minute; hung around with enough flyboys that I know my shit."

"Why don't you join up, then?"

"I was, once upon a time, a private in the 42nd in 1918," Patrick answered. "I don't think FDR wants a 40-year-old with trench foot doing his fighting for him."

"You never mentioned you fought in the Great War," Thomas said.

"Never actually saw much frontline in France. Got to Europe at the end of October, stood in the trenches long enough for my feet to nearly rot off, then the war was over November 11. Afterwards, I *did* enjoy the services of some of France's best brothels-a teenage kid has to become a man at some point."

Thomas damn near spit out his coffee with laughter as he imagined Patrick's twenty seconds of joy with some poor French farmgirl. "Pilot it is, then."

"Think about it-you sleep in a warm bed every night and have hot chow three meals a day. Probably even get some hazard pay out of it."

"Maybe even do some fighting while I'm in one of those planes, too."

The two swapped stories and listened to more details about the barbaric attack on the Hawaiian Islands for hours, and not a soul entered the bar. It seemed everyone in Santa Monica and the rest of the country was glued to their radio as America was now involved in the global conflict it had spent the past few years avoiding. As the hours wore on, Thomas realized he best be going if he was going to enlist in the morning. Life as he knew it was about to change dramatically.

"Do you mind if I use your phone to call my parents in San Diego before I leave?" he asked, knowing the answer, but wanting to be polite anyway.

"Absolutely, kid, let your mom and pop know you're okay and that you're signing up tomorrow to avenge the boys in Hawaii."

The phone rang only once before Matthew answered the phone. "Hello?" he asked nervously. He had clearly heard the news and knew the country was under attack.

"Dad, it's me, Thomas."

"Good to hear from you, son! Have you heard the news about Pearl Harbor? Absolutely horrible."

"I did, and I want to do something about it."

"Are you signing up?"

"Yes, sir," he began, figuring now was as good a time as any to get used to military lingo and terminology. "I want to be a pilot."

"That's great news, son. If you have the chance to see us before you ship out to training, please do. It would mean the world to your mother and me."

"I will," Thomas said. He gently hung up the phone as a tear dripped down his face. He knew he wasn't the ideal son for his parents, but they loved and supported him, regardless of his antics. Now, he was determined to reward their faith and love in him by showing he was much more than the sum of his parts.

Returning to Patrick and the radio, he asked, "Do you think the Japs would invade California?"

"I hope they're that stupid. You don't know it, but there's a 12-gauge that I know how to use in that far cabinet behind a few tequila bottles. Myself and every other gun owner on the West Coast would have the Jap Army backpedaling all the way to fucking Tokyo before the Army and the Marines even got here."

"You seem optimistic about an easy victory."

"They're Japs, for Christ's sake. And they've got no idea who they just picked a fight with. Name a war this country's lost. You can't. Hell, we've got my old commander with the 42nd, General MacArthur, and his boys in the Philippines, too. They'll probably do the bulk of the fighting and give us an easy place to invade Japan from."

"My cousin Brian's over there, serving in General MacArthur's staff. He graduated from West Point last June," Thomas said, proud of his cousin's accomplishments but nervous that he was now in harm's way, thousands of miles from the U.S. mainland.

"Lucky guy. He'll probably be in Tokyo cutting the Emperor's balls off and feeding them to him before you even finish basic."

"God willing," Thomas said as he shook Patrick's hand and made his way out the door.

"Take care of yourself, kid. Come here after the war for a round on me when you get home."

As Thomas walked away, he couldn't help but laugh, "*You're* buying a round? Holy fuck! Then I'll have to come back alive so I can say I witnessed a miracle. I'll settle for still having a job when I get back."

"I'll give you one of the two—dealer's choice—when you get your ass back here."

Thomas didn't get his beauty sleep the night of December 7. His tossing and turning meant he only got a few short hours of shuteye before he went to the armed forces recruiting station.

At 6:30 a.m., Thomas rubbed the sleep out his eyes, quickly downed a cup of coffee, and rode to the recruitment station in what he thought would be plenty of time. As he rolled up to the station, he couldn't believe his eyes—countless young men had camped out overnight in hopes of signing up.

"Guess I'm not the only one that wants to kick some ass," he said as he got in line, planning to be there for a long time.

It was almost noon by the time Thomas got to a recruiter's desk, by then, he was extra antsy.

He was sent for a medical evaluation, where all the essentials were done by a clearly well-fed doctor and a pretty Navy nurse. Things were going extremely well—he was still in stellar shape from his college days and his recent introduction to surfing, until the doctor felt something wrong with his wrist.

"Son, your wrist isn't exactly what we'd call A-1," the doctor said, as he stamped a big 'F' on his physical report.

Thomas knew his troublesome wrist wasn't exactly in stellar shape, but it hadn't hindered anything since that fateful play in the Rose Bowl. "It's just fine, sir. Let me pass, so I can kill some Japs from an airplane, the way they did to our boys on the Arizona."

"You're 4-F. You can help the war effort just the same from the homefront."

"Look, I need to be *there*. I'm not about to be some beta male who lets someone else do my fighting for me."

"It's not *your* fighting—it's the United States of America's fighting. And we don't need you and your gimpy wrist to kill the Japs," he said, as he dismissed Thomas and called the next recruit. "NEXT!"

"Fuck this," Thomas said as he stormed away from the man who, in his eyes, was deliberately robbing him of glory.

"That attitude doesn't fly in the military, son. You probably wouldn't get through basic, anyway," the portly doctor said, getting one last jab in.

To say Thomas was devastated as he walked out of the recruiting office was the understatement of the century. America was at war, as not only had Hawaii been bombed, but

Guam, some outpost called Wake Island, and Brian's post in the Philippines had all fallen under attack that day. Staying at home wasn't an option. "I need a drink," he said as he got back on his Harley with no destination in mind.

He didn't want Patrick to know he'd been turned down, so instead of heading for Junction, he rode south toward San Diego, where maybe his parents would have a clearer answer for him. His father had plenty of pull in seemingly every facet of life, but did he have *enough* pull to get his 4-F overturned and get him in the air, shooting down Zeroes?

He pulled into the family's home in Encinitas during the mid-afternoon and looked out at the vastness of the Pacific. Somewhere on the other side of the never-ending green and blue, there was a war going on, and he wanted—no, needed—to get involved.

"Fancy seeing you here," Matthew said as he greeted his son in the driveway.

"Stupid military doctor said I'm 4-F and unfit for service because of my wrist. I didn't know where else to come."

"I told you after that game to get it looked at it, but you were fine with being in pain. As usual, you always knew better than everyone else. I tell you, sometimes you make a damn mule seem agreeable."

"Can you talk to your friend, Dr. Porter, about giving me a pass to go over? He was in the Navy and has some pull."

"We're spending Christmas with Dr. and Mrs. Porter in Palm Springs. You're welcome to join us. You can talk to him yourself out there."

"So, I have to wait three weeks before I can even get looked at? What if we're in Tokyo by then?"

"God willing, this war will be long over before you have the chance to get in an airplane and be in harm's way," said Matthew, who brightened at the prospect of his son never seeing active duty. "Besides, Dr. Porter and his wife are in Chicago right now. They won't even be back in California for another two weeks."

"C'mon! You served in Russia back in the day—it'd be un-American for me not to join in the fray."

"Fine. I'll ask Dr. Porter to look at your wrist in Palm Springs just before Christmas and tell him how much you want to serve. In the meantime, make yourself useful around here. I'll be short workers due to enlistments, and I can use all the help I can get."

"A Whitney working the line at Whitney Shipbuilding? War does make crazy things happen," Thomas said with a smile. "What're we going to do to stay in business during the war with all the men off fighting the Huns?"

"Old men, and dare I say, even women, will be working the line, keeping us in business and putting ships in the water."

"Talk about a change of pace," Thomas said as he imagined the war ships that the factories would now be turning out to help bring the Japanese to their knees.

"That's why I'm home so early. I shut the factory down for the day. Wasn't worth trying to get so much work done with such a skeleton crew. Come on inside; your Mother made a nice shepherd's pie that I'm sure can feed at least three people. Roosevelt's speech is being replayed on the radio. Did you hear it?"

"No, I missed it. Any good?"

"Actually, yes. I may not be a fan of the guy, but he's one hell of an orator, and we need leadership at the top at times like this."

Roosevelt may or may not have been the right guy to lead the country to war, but Thomas knew he was the perfect guy for a supporting role in the unfriendly skies. In Thomas's mind, he was the round peg in the round hole. Not everyone can be a headliner, but Thomas wanted to play his part in the grand scheme of things.

***

Palm Springs, California

December 24, 1941

Palm Springs has always been the desert playground for California's elite, and through the decades, that hasn't changed. But the Christmas of 1941 didn't exactly breed hope and good will toward all mankind in this oasis. In the weeks since Pearl Harbor, the Japanese had landed in Guam, the Philippines, Wake Island, and the British colonies of Hong Kong and Malaya and had the allies on the run. Hopes for an easy victory had gone right out the window as the Japanese seemed to be smarter, better prepared, and more tenacious an enemy than America had seen in her history. To add insult to injury, the U.S. had declared war on Germany and Italy and war on two fronts was about to be a reality.

Despite all this, Thomas couldn't wait to see Dr. Porter—he held Thomas's key to the skies. Dr. Steven Porter was Matthew Whitney's golfing buddy, and, over the years, they'd grown close over their love of the sport. Prior to going into private practice in San Diego, Dr. Porter was one of the U.S. Navy's most respected surgeons, and he still had pull within the armed forces. If his signature was attached to a physical, then it was good as gold. He didn't have a surgeon's table to examine Thomas's wrist on, but the kitchen table at the Whitneys' rental home would do.

Dr. Porter didn't want to be the bearer of bad news, but in his time in the profession, he had grown accustomed to it. "Son, I wish you had let me look at this when the injury happened. This wrist has never healed right. But 4-F isn't as bad as it sounds. You can serve at home and still help the war effort."

"Fuck that."

"I beg your pardon, son?" a shocked Dr. Porter answered. He wasn't used to such crass language from his patients, and it was especially unexpected from the son of Matthew and Katlyn.

"We've got the biggest war in the history of the planet going on, and I want in. And by in' I don't mean diddling myself as a civil servant in Oklahoma or working as a foreman at my father's plant. I know my body better than anyone else does, and I know I have what it takes. I can handle the pain—it won't hold me back."

Dr. Porter realized he was in a losing fight, and rather than let it drag it on, he relented.

"Fine, I'll set you up with my friend Dr. Harbaugh in Los Angeles. He knows a thing or two about patching up wrists. I'm sure he can fit you into his docket just after the New Year and have you in training not too long after that. You'll have to pay out-of-pocket, and there's still absolutely no guarantee your wrist survives training, much less the war, but his work on it should be enough to pass the military's inconsistent standards."

"Money is no issue—I'll pay whatever it takes to get out there and avenge those boys on the Arizona," replied Thomas, with his hope restored. "I appreciate it, Doc. I'll credit you with *some* of the Japs I kill."

"We're at war with Germany and Italy, too; there's no guarantee you'll be sent to the Pacific," Dr. Porter said, giving the young man a quick current affairs lesson.

"I've got no beef with Hitler or Mussolini; in fact, we should join up with them to take out the Russians and that fuck, Joe Stalin after we beat Japan like a drum."

"We're on the same team as Russia now; you can't be speaking like that. I'm sure you had teammates over your years of athletic prowess that you didn't see eye-to-eye with."

"This is different," Thomas said, failing to realize he was talking to a well-traveled, well-educated doctor who had served in the military.

"Well, son, you don't dictate the terms of the world, and if I'm going to pass you on to Dr. Harbaugh, it's on the basis of your willingness to rid the world of tyranny and oppression—and your confused ideals. Don't make me regret this decision before you have the surgery."

Thomas didn't completely agree with what the doctor was saying, but he would have agreed with just about anything if it meant getting to the front. "Yes, sir."

"What's the verdict, Doc?" Matthew Whitney asked, as Porter and the soon-to-be pilot left the guest house and entered the area around the swimming pool.

"Your son will be a mile high, raining hell from above in no time," said Porter. "My colleague in Los Angeles will perform surgery on him after the New Year. I'll take the liberty of making the arrangements for the boy between now and then."

"Good. You can enjoy the holiday with us, then sign up to fight," said Matthew. "God knows there'll be plenty of war to fight, and Lord only knows when you'll be able to spend Christmas at home again."

Thomas had gotten exactly what he wanted for Christmas. In the true spirit of Christmas, he knew he'd be giving, not receiving, when he got his marching orders, and the enemy would be getting the type of present that isn't on a list. Right now, however, he could only imagine what lay ahead for him.

Unknown Location between Besançon and the Swiss Border

October 15, 1943

1705 hours

Sundown was near, and neither Thomas nor Rebecca had heard even a footstep from a German patrol. They were far from safety, but apparently, the German army had bigger fish to fry on this particular afternoon than to chase a refugee and a downed pilot.

"When do you want to get moving again?" Rebecca asked Thomas as he awoke from his latest thirty-minute siesta.

"Once it gets dark. I want to get the fuck out of here," Thomas said, even though the second part of his answer was obvious. Why would anyone want to keep sleeping on a rock on a cold evening in rural France with enemy troops looking to kill them?

"While you were sleeping, I took a look at your map," she said, unfolding it and showing him. "If we stay parallel to this road that runs east, then by sunrise, we should be only one night's march from Switzerland."

"Thirty-six hours from safety. I can get behind that idea."

"Well, the Swiss border is heavily guarded by German and Swiss troops. I don't have any papers, and you're a uniformed soldier, so there are no guarantees."

"So, we can't just walk into Switzerland?"

"No, we'll need to sneak in and go from there. My sister is in Bern, thirty kilometers from the border. She can help me and her home. Or at least, where I remember her home being is not far from the American Embassy."

"If we're lucky."

"Let's stop bickering about Switzerland and worry about actually getting there," Rebecca said, knowing there was no guarantee they'd even sniff the border.

Thomas picked himself up off the ground and got ready to move. Speed would be important, but maintaining a silent presence under the nose of countless enemy troops would be the difference between getting to the border and being imprisoned in a camp. Much like he was taught in flight school, there had to be a happy medium between being fast and being shifty, and for a split second, in the autumn evening of southwest France, he longed to be back in flight school, where in the woods of Alabama, he learned what little he knew about escape and evasion.

"Why did you become a pilot?" Rebecca asked as they began their cold march.

"I wanted to be a daredevil—be the guy that saved the day at just right moment. I also thought I'd be able to sleep in a bed every night and get three hot meals every day. I might have been wrong about that one."

"Life isn't perfect," she shrugged. "What was pilot training like? They don't just let you get behind the controls of a plane and take it into battle, do they?"

"God, no. They trained us well and good before we went into battle." Thomas thought, given his situation, that he wasn't sure he'd had *enough* training.

Thomas couldn't help but think of just how much had changed since he first became an aviator at a small base in the rural south. It was a world away, but in some ways, it was almost too eerily similar to his present, sparse surroundings.

***

November 12, 1942

Montgomery, Alabama

Maxwell Army Air Force Base was a world away from what Thomas was used to. The southeast United States might as well have been a foreign country for a man born in California and partially educated in New England. The "Whites Only" signs were just another reminder that the "United" in United States still wasn't completely accurate. The landscape couldn't have been any more different than California either, as rocky hills gave way to tree after tree after tree, and the ocean was nothing more than a distant thought. Even so, Thomas was happy to be able to train so he could hopefully use his expertise and daredevil attitude to slay the bastards who had bombed Pearl Harbor and conquered the Philippines. He had finished his basic training and officer candidate school, but this is where it became real. How he performed in flight school would determine whether he spent the war flying or on the ground, doing grunt work.

Sitting alone in his top bunk, he was greeted by the fellow trainee who took the bottom.

"Tyler Donovan," the young man said in a New England accent, eagerly reaching up to shake Thomas's hand. "Nice to meet you."

"Thomas Whitney-you as well. Where are you from?"

"Massachusetts. You?"

"San Diego, California. Went to high school in New England for a year, though."

"Where at?"

"Deerfield Academy. Played football there before going to USC."

"No shit! I wanted to go there, but I didn't have the money and just missed out on a scholarship. I played at Needham High School then went to Bryant University. Didn't play ball there, though."

"I played public school ball for three years in California. No shame in it," Thomas said, the entitlement from his upper-class upbringing shining through like a lighthouse on the coast.

"How'd you end up joining the Air Corps?" Lieutenant Donovan asked as he tried like hell to move the conversation toward a topic that would make his bunkmate seem at least somewhat likeable.

"Wanted to bring death from above to the bad guys. How about you?"

"It's probably the only job in the military I have any experience with. I flew a crop-duster in Western Massachusetts during the summer to help pay for college. Might as well crop-dust some Krauts."

"I'm hoping we go to the Pacific, I've got no issues with Hitler; hell, I'd take him over Uncle Joe Stalin any day of the week," Thomas said as his unadulterated hatred of communism-even if it meant praising an enemy of America-shone through yet again.

"Isn't bad-mouthing an ally something the military generally frowns upon?" said Tyler, taken aback as he suspiciously looked Thomas up and down.

"He's not *my* ally—he's a murderous villain that should be hung by his balls in Times Square."

Tyler was once again stunned. The two would surely end up going to war together and would need to have each others' backs, but this rhetoric was something he wasn't expecting. Tyler wasn't the type to pick political arguments—he was truly a "go along to get along" kind of guy—the polar opposite of this idealistic, opinionated flyboy.

"Well, I'm just here to serve my country and go home. Go where they want me to go, kill who they want me to kill, and then go back to Massachusetts."

"What kind of work is waiting for you in Massachusetts?" Thomas asked, ready to change the subject.

"I was selling insurance before the war, or trying to, anyway. I'll probably do something like that once this whole nightmare comes to an end."

"Sounds like a really great time," Thomas grunted, a hint of sarcasm pushing through.

"Are you always this much of an asshole, or is this just a way to make a memorable first impression?" Tyler asked, getting sick of his bunkmate's pointless, ball-busting attitude.

"If I piss you off enough, and you harness your anger toward fighting the enemy, then we'll have this war won in no time."

"One way or another, it'll seem like an eternity," Tyler said as he settled into his bottom bunk. They got ready for the first round of on-the-ground training before they could take to the skies.

On the second day of flight training, Tyler and Thomas came face-to-face with the vehicle that would define their war. The bunkmates and the rest of their training group were herded into one of the base's many hangers where the unveiling would happen. The brass was here, and the entire unit waited silently before someone in a dress uniform got up in front of the group to address them.

"Pilots like you will be the reason this war will be won," said the colonel, whose name nobody quite heard. "Every minute of training will help you to slay the enemies that look to enslave the free world and end liberty as we all know it."

"I thought Howard Jones's pep talks sucked," whispered Thomas, recalling his former coach at the University of Southern California, "but this guy takes it to an entirely new level." Lieutenant Donovan, ever the student, ignored him and kept taking notes.

"The best instrument you pilots will have is your brain, but the factory workers of America have gifted you another instrument with which to do battle. I introduce to you, gentlemen, the P-51 Mustang. The Nips and Krauts think they own the skies over their respective battlefields, but you select pilots will be the ones who remind them just how sorely they are mistaken."

"That is sexier than Rita Hayworth," Tyler remarked, in awe of this new American-made machinery.

"Oh my Lord, I can only imagine the damage I'll do when we finally get over there," Thomas, ever the braggadocious gem, said, imagining himself becoming every Japanese fighter's worst nightmare.

As the days and weeks in Alabama wore on, Thomas's already high confidence level soared with every sortie over the southern skies. While it may have been training, and there was no enemy looking to end his or his fellow trainees' lives, flying a piece of machinery that weighed almost five tons through the heavens was no small task. Tyler was excellent on the control sticks, and his intelligence and attention to detail separated him from almost the whole class. The two opposites complemented each other perfectly, and it was apparent to their superiors that they represented the very best of this year's cohort of new American aviators. The night before flight school graduation, the colonel-whose name they now knew-summoned them into his office.

"Colonel Nardi, you wanted to see us, sir?" Tyler asked nervously as the pair of aviators stood before their commanding officer. Despite being the definition of a straight-arrow, Tyler still got paranoid any time he was summoned by a superior. Growing up with an Irish-Catholic mother would do that.

"I did," the Colonel began. "You're the two best fliers in your class. You've taken what you've learned in training to heart and applied your own internal strengths. Your work here has been a testament to yourselves, your family, and your country. So, you both have options."

"Options, sir?" Thomas replied.

"Yes. You can both go over and shoot down enemy fighters, or stay here and work as instructors. As much as we need our best and brightest in the skies, we also need capable teachers to ensure that every pilot who comes through here is ready for the real action. The decision is up to the two of you—you can both stay, you can both go, or you can split up. All up to you."

"I signed up to fight, sir," replied Thomas confidently. "Besides, if you'd seen how horrible I was at teaching English, you wouldn't want me instructing anyone. I appreciate it, Sir, but I've already turned down the option to stay stateside once. I want in on the fight."

"Noted," Nardi said to Thomas, jotting down his answer on a sheet of paper. He turned to Tyler. "Lieutenant Donovan?"

As much as being an instructor in Alabama and not being shot out of the sky by a German or Japanese pilot sounded intriguing, Tyler just couldn't do it. Part of it was his desire to serve his country, but the other part came from not wanting to be outdone by Thomas. He didn't have the same arrogant exterior as the California native, but he too had an internal self-confidence that drove him. "I want to go overseas, too, sir."

"I understand. It's a shame to lose you, but there's a war to be won, and having the two of you in the sky will help make that a reality."

"Sir, since we placed so high in our class, do we have any say in where we'll be stationed?" Thomas chimed in, hoping to use his excellence in the skies to leverage a spot in the Pacific theatre.

"The Army doesn't work like that, Lieutenant Whitney. This isn't an auction block where you can bid for what you want. You go where you're told to go, and in the rare case you're given an option, take advantage of it. If that's everything then you're dismissed, and I will see the two of you tomorrow at graduation."

The two young lieutenants saluted and made their way out of the room.

"Leveraging a ranking officer? I've seen it all, Whit," Tyler said, as his unbelievably opportunistic partner continued to amaze him.

"There are coconut drinks and avenging Pearl Harbor on one hand or dreary Europe and having to fight on the same side as Stalin on the other. You can't blame a man for trying."

"Will you shut up about Stalin?" Tyler replied with an eye-roll.

"I'm against tyranny, and Stalin is the definition of tyrannical. You being so smart should know that. Speaking of which, I'm shocked you didn't stay behind to teach the next generation of pilots."

"I wonder if it's too late to change my mind," Tyler said as they made their way outside.

"There's no guarantee we're stationed together. The Army might see fit to break us up, which would be a damn tragedy."

"I've accepted the fact that I'm not that lucky, and we'll be together for the duration—a fate that may be worse than actual death," Tyler said with *just* a bit of hyperbole.

***

Occupied France, 50 Miles from Switzerland

October 16, 1943

0130 hours

Walking blindly through the woods of France with nothing more than a pair of handguns, and a "partner" anything but suited to carrying a gun, was not how Thomas Whitney planned on spending the war. His own shooting skills left a lot to be desired, but this frail girl, barely old enough to have a drink, had clearly never held a gun. He thought to himself, at one point, that it might be better for him to double-fist the pistols like daiquiris on the beach, since at least he had fired one before. That thought quickly dissipated as he thought back to the first time he fired a pistol—with only a hand on the grip and a finger on the trigger like a cowboy in the old west; the kickback planted him on his backside. From then on, it was two hands on the trigger like the handbook said. The naturally right-handed Thomas needed to use his left as his strong hand when he used his gun because that nagging wrist injury really came back to him when he pulled the trigger. Either way, they would be absolutely screwed if they ran into a unit of heavily-armed German soldiers, but spreading the wealth in terms of weaponry at least gave them a chance. Even if she didn't hit anything, maybe the Germans would keep their heads down, and the two of them could slip away.

"Stop," Rebecca just audibly whispered as they came upon a dirt road with fresh tracks on it—likely from a German tank.

Thomas ducked and pulled his old-school revolver out, ready to grease the first thing that came within range. Given the limited capabilities of his weapon, any bad guy would have to be pretty damn close in order to be *in range*.

"The coast is clear," the young woman said as the two kept moving eastward.

"How did you know to stop and when to get going again?" Thomas asked Rebecca, who clearly lacked any semblance of training but also had a keen sense of situational awareness. He had gone through escape and evasion training, but even he would have likely missed the tank tracks on the dirt road until it was too late had Rebecca not alerted him.

"It's about taking the extra second to look and think. Contrary to what you may think, brawn isn't everything—brains need to be involved, too," Rebecca calmly and quietly said, without breaking her stride on the other side of the dirt road. "Blindly walking across that road without taking the split second could have left us exposed."

Thomas's jaw damn near hit the ground. He'd had briefings and some training on what to do as a downed aviator in occupied territory, but never had it been laid out so clearly for him. "You remind me of someone I know, or rather someone I knew," Thomas said.

"Who is that?" she quietly asked, wary of possible enemies in the occupied territory.

"My bunkmate and wingman, Tyler, who got shot down yesterday, too. He wasn't as lucky as I was."

"Did he get tired of your antics, too?"

Thomas thought her question was crass at first, but realized that she, too, just suffered a great loss. Her question wasn't sugar-coated with bullshit—it was honest, and he respected that. "As a matter of fact, I grew on him."

***

New York, New York

August 7, 1943

"We can still be shipped across the country to join the Pacific war effort, right?" Thomas asked Tyler as they looked at New York Harbor.

"I don't know why the Army would ship us to Manhattan with a ticket across the Atlantic, only to reroute us to California," Tyler said as his patience—one of his greatest strengths—was wearing *just* a little thin.

"Nothing the Army does makes any sense, so it *could* happen," Thomas said, trying to speak a one-way ticket to the Pacific into existence.

"New York City isn't so bad. You seem to be enjoying yourself," Tyler said as his obnoxiously West Coast partner eyed a Big Apple citizen of the opposite sex walking by.

"Girls love a man in uniform," Thomas said, his mind shifting from frustration to his pleasant memories of their brief time in Manhattan.

"If that's the case, you should have been a mailman. I hear girls go crazy for those uniforms," Tyler said. He loved to humble his overly arrogant partner.

Thomas, as per usual, just brushed off his buddy's criticism and thought ahead to what Britain would be like. "Think the broads in London will feel the same way about our uniforms?"

Tyler just shook his head and rolled his eyes at Thomas. "I'm sure the fine young ladies of the British Isles will be crazy for a handsome American man in a U.S. Army uniform. Hell, they might even elect you prime minister while we're there."

"Sounds like a nice gig. Downing Street hasn't seen anything like me before," Thomas said as he thought more and more about what was to come.

"I hate saying this, but I'm glad we're shipping out together," Tyler said, as he took another sip of martini. "It might be the gin talking, but you're an alright guy, most of the time."

"You're alright, too," said Thomas. "But we've got to stick together over there."

Tyler nodded. Thomas continued.

"Those boys in the Eighth have been in the fight a while, so we'll be joining as replacements," Thomas said, hoping his and Tyler's differences would bring them together and serve them well in combat. "We need to prove ourselves early and often. Teamwork is the best way to do that."

They didn't get the assignment he wanted, but Thomas Whitney would get to fight. There was a troop ship in New York harbor that would bring him and Tyler to Britain, where their shiny new P-51s would be waiting for them. When he boiled it down to the bare bones, there was nowhere else he'd rather be and not another pilot in the army he'd rather be flying with. They were mere weeks away from the skies over Europe and less than twenty-four hours away from leaving American soil. There was a chance this would be their last night ever spent in the country they had signed up to defend, and that realization was sobering no matter how many gin martinis they put down.

***

August 17, 1943

Honington, England

For all the ribbing and, at times, pure bullshit that came from Thomas's mouth, Tyler came to like him, and they quickly became attached at the hip, with the drunken confession in New York being a microcosm of his feelings. They had missed an earlier operation in North Africa and Italy and were joining the fight in England as the unfortunate replacements, but they were still anxious to join the fighting.

"This is such fucking bullshit that we have to be over here," Thomas said as he and Tyler walked onto their new home in the British Isles. "I want to kill Japs, not Germans."

"Tom, I've listened to you complain ever since we got our marching orders in New Jersey last month. I get it," Tyler said, *this close* from slapping his wingman from one end of the British Isles to another. "We're in England now—we're here to win the war in Europe, and that's that. Stop acting like an entitled brat with a silver spoon up his ass."

"When did you become the world's ultimate hardass?"

"Somewhere in the middle of the North Atlantic, when I decided throwing you overboard and spending the war in Leavenworth wasn't worth it and that I was stuck with you for better or for worse, like a deranged marriage."

"Shame, I hear the accommodations are better than they are over here," Thomas said. The Kansas military prison was anything but a high-end estate, but their new bunks seemed worse.

Before the two could finish their usual argument, they spotted a ranking officer making a beeline toward them. Their conversation ceased, and they were standing at attention by the time he stood before them.

"Afternoon gentlemen. I'm Major Leney. You two are...?"

"Lieutenant Donovan, Tyler."

"Lieutenant Whitney, Thomas."

"Yes, my newest pilots—fresh out of Maxwell. Nice to meet you, gentlemen. I'm your commanding officer. Get yourself situated and report to my office ASAP so I can get you guys up to speed and up in the air sooner rather than later."

"Yes, sir," they both replied, as their commanding officer walked away with the same speed and focus he had approached them with.

"He'll be fun to fly with," Thomas said sarcastically. He reminded him of every hard-assed teacher he'd ever had.

"I can't wait until the first time you *really* piss him off by being your usual moronic self," Tyler fired back. Once again, Thomas couldn't go a full minute without saying something stupid.

"We're in a war zone, I'm all business right now. No time for games."

"I'm not sure if they teach biology in California, but I learned once upon a time that leopards don't change their spots."

"That's zoology, by the way," Thomas shot back. "Sorry your parents couldn't afford private school."

"You're such an asshole," Tyler replied as he was learning to let Thomas' sarcasm and ball busting not get to him.

The two walked into the major's office and saw it was put together with the precision and attention to detail that would come from a West Point graduate.

"Welcome to England, gentlemen. I'll keep it short and sweet: our mission here is to provide fighter support for the flying fortresses, to make sure they get to and from their targets in one piece. We mainly launch our raids during the day; the Brits fly at night. The higher-ups view the 24/7 bombing as the key to softening Europe for an eventual cross-Channel invasion. When that will happen, God only knows, but we're here to make sure it's a smashing success as soon as it does. Am I clear?"

"Yes, sir," the duo answered.

"Alright, get yourselves set up in the barracks, and I'll see you back here at fifteen hundred for a briefing. After that, you'll be introduced to the planes you'll be flying," Leney told them. "If you haven't noticed yet, your cherries are getting popped tomorrow morning, first thing."

Tyler and Thomas were the very definition of fresh-faced combat virgins, but for Major Leney and others who had been in the theatre of operations for a while, sorties over occupied France had become an almost monotonous part of the job.

Tyler and Thomas obviously knew the gist of their mission before they arrived in Britain, but the major was clearly a by-the-book officer that would rather overstate a point then leave anything up to chance. They knew he was a career soldier who believed deeply, not only in the goals of the unit's assignments, but in the U.S. Army as a whole. Unlike the pair of aviators, this was his calling, and war or no war, there was no place he'd rather be than serving the United States Army.

Walking into the briefing room, the two rookies saw what being in theatre for almost a year had done to the veteran pilots. Rather than talking and joking, like Thomas and Tyler did in basic, their new squad-mates sat quietly and awaited Leney's arrival with their instructions. Rather than make introductions before the briefing, Tyler and Thomas sat down in the back and added to the sound of deafening silence.

"ATTENTION!"

A voice that sounded like and turned out to be Leney's sounded out as the whole unit rose to their feet with their commanding officer entering the room. As Leney walked down the mini-aisle between the seats, the pilots stood at attention. "As you were, gentlemen," Leney said in a manner that was *almost* casual.

This was yet another part of military doctrine that Thomas didn't fully understand. "Why do we bother standing up when we have to sit right back down? What's the end game with exercises in futility like that?" he thought to himself. All he wanted to do was break some of the tension, and he needed to wait for his perfect moment.

"We're calling this Operation Mermaid. Your objective will be…" Major Leney began as he pointed to a map in front of his group of pilots.

Thomas saw his window to be the class clown and interrupted the major mid-sentence.

"Sir, is it taking place under the sea?"

Sure enough, his fellow fighters, including Lieutenant Donovan, were laughing like a pack of hyenas at the new wisenheimer of the unit. Whatever tension there may have been between the veterans and the new rookies was not to be, as Thomas's wisecrack put everybody at ease.

"No, lieutenant, it is not taking place under the sea," Major Leney said, as he gave Thomas the look that every parent has ever given their child right before grounding them into the next decade. "Rather, above the sea, on the port city of Le Havre, France. There are some German warships docked there, and Ike would like to sink them like the damn Titanic. Enemy airpower in the area appears to be light, so we *should* have the job done before they can scramble anything, but you never know with the Luftwaffe. You guys that have been here for a while know the drill—the new guys will pick up on it. Let the bombers do their thing, make sure they get back okay, and don't try to be a hero and take on the whole Luftwaffe. Everyone but Whitney is dismissed."

"Way to make a first impression, moron," Tyler said to Thomas as he left the room, leaving his buddy to the wrath of their superior.

"I think he likes me and wants to be friends," Thomas replied as Tyler and the rest of their squad filed out. He knew his ass was about to be grass, and the major was the lawnmower.

Thomas walked up to Major Leney, who was standing, almost fully relaxed, at the front of the room, waiting for him. "You wanted to see me, sir?"

"Look, lieutenant, you've barely been here for a minute, and you're already on my shit list. You want to be the jokester? That's fine—do it on your time—but don't *ever* undermine one of my briefings ever again," he said sternly. "It's my job to make sure as many of you as possible get home in one piece. Hot dogging in the briefings means information doesn't get across, and he less you guys know, the more likely some schnitzel-eater will blow you or one of your buddies out of the sky. I doubt you want that on your conscience."

Then he got even more serious.

"You pull that shit again, and you'll be peeling potatoes in the kitchen while the rest of he unit is flying and killing Krauts. Understood?"

"Yes, sir," Thomas said as he stood stone-faced in front of his commander. He had done what he could to get to this point, and while it wasn't avenging Pearl Harbor, he wasn't about to et his clownery keep him from making a difference. Besides, this wasn't training in Alabama or New Jersey—this was the real deal, and lives could be put at risk by his antics.

"Good. Now get the fuck out of my sight."

Tyler and a few of the airmen he wasn't formally introduced to were waiting to hear the gossip. "Is he sending you back stateside to fly cattle across state lines?" Tyler asked.

"Nope, gave me a warning and told me to cut the shit. If I had a dime for every time I heard that growing up, I'd be richer than my old man."

"Of course," Tyler sighed. He turned to the two flyboys standing beside him. "This is Lieutenant Danny Edelman, and this is Lieutenant Robert Gorman."

"It's an honor, gentlemen," Thomas said, shaking their hands.

"That was some funny shit," said Gorman with a laugh. "We need that from time to time around here. Don't worry about the major—he's got a stick so far up his ass, the very end of it is his nose."

"Career soldiers—you know how they get," Edelman added.

"So, where are you boys from?" Thomas asked.

"I'm from Texas, and this guy is from Ohio," Danny Edelman began. "Your boy tells us you were a college ball player?"

"Yes, University of Southern California. You play any ball?"

"I played a little bit of baseball for the Longhorns, mostly second base, a little outfield here and there. I was too short to play football," the five-foot-nothing, hundred-and-nothing Edelman said.

"I was on the varsity drinking team at Ohio University. I drank my way through Dublin more times than I could ever care to count. My only touchdowns came from nights with the finest sorority sisters on campus," Lieutenant Gorman said, as he thought of his days as a Bobcat in the Buckeye State.

"Sounds like we'll all get along just fine. Don't mind him, he's a straight arrow—we'll get him crooked in no time," Thomas said, referring to Tyler's more civilized personality, but leaving out that Lieutenant Donovan had no issue taking a drink himself.

"Stick with us when we're in formation up there," Gorman said. "We'll get you home okay."

"How long have you boys been over here?"

"Got to England a few weeks ago. Before that, we flew in North Africa and the Mediterranean," Gorman said. "We've been around the block a time or two."

"I'll say. What's this target we're hitting tomorrow morning?" Tyler said as he wanted all the information he could get about this target.

"It's a U-Boat hub that we've bombed before. They keep rebuilding, and we keep bombing—it's a vicious cycle," Edelman said. Their missions had been at least somewhat successful, but the Germans always rebuilt what the American and British pilots had destroyed.

"Any civilians in the area?" Lieutenant Donovan chimed in.

"Unfortunately, yes. The bombers have dropped their payloads on everything in the town, and sadly, that means civilians, too," Danny said. He knew collateral damage was a fact of life and wanted the rookie flyers to understand that sooner rather than later.

"Bottom line is, just be there if the Luftwaffe scrambles any fighters, watch your six, follow our lead, and we'll be back in time for lunch," Lieutenant Gorman added.

"Where's the hangar?" asked Thomas. "I want to at least meet this fine lady before I fuck her." Thomas grinned at the men around him.

"Usually, Leney does that introductions, but since he's probably behind his desk seething at Lieutenant Whitney's very existence, I'll take on that honor," said Gorman. "Follow me." Lieutenant Gorman led his two rookies out of the room, who tailed him like dogs following an owner with a piece of steak.

The trio walked about a hundred yards down tarmac and came to two new P-51s. To the rookies, they looked like new toys under a Christmas tree. These amazing pieces of aviation excellence were built on a line, put on a ship, and delivered to waiting aviators.

"I'll be damned. She's even more beautiful than I imagined," Thomas quipped as he looked the plane up and down like the work of art it was.

"Fresh out of the box. Can't wait to see how it handles over there," Tyler said as he ran his hand across the metallic hull. The armor-plated exterior was tough, but just how much *care* the factory workers put into making the plane would be obvious when they took to the not-so-friendly skies.

"You'll get your chance tomorrow morning with the rest of the squadron," Lieutenant Gorman said as he brought the rookies back to earth. The machines may have been beautiful, but they were instruments of war, and they'd be going into harm's way while they were behind the stick.

"Can we paint logos on the plane?" Lieutenant Donovan asked excitedly. He may not have had Thomas's never-ending, self-serving vanity, but he wanted to put his own personal mark on his plane.

"Unwritten rule here is you have to fly three combat missions before you get to paint your plane. Given how busy we are, you'll probably reach that milestone by the end of the week. You have to prove you're one of us before you add any color to your bird."

"Roger that," Thomas answered. He'd been part of so many rituals on his teams over the years that, if anything, this just made him feel closer to home.

"Spend some time with the planes, but don't forget to get yourselves some sleep. We've got a big one ahead of us tomorrow," Lieutenant Gorman said as he began walking away.

"Will do. See you guys tomorrow morning," Thomas said as he and Tyler took one last look at their planes. They retired to their quarters shortly after.

Neither one could sleep. The thought of combat kept them awake all night. It was the fear of potentially dying, mixed with the anticipation of Christmas Eve. "What do you think it'll be like up there?" Thomas asked a praying Tyler.

"Dangerous? Scary? I don't know, man."

"Are those rosary beads?" Thomas asked, his head poking down to take a peek at his bunkmate.

"They are. My mom and dad had the parish priest bless them and then mailed them to me."

"Since when have you been religious?"

"Since I realized there's a chance my aircraft—filled with God knows how much low-quality gas—could be shot down, and I could be burned to a crisp a mile up by an enemy that gets off on that kind of stuff," Tyler said as he laid his head down on his pillow.

"I'm not a huge prayer guy. Either the Krauts are gonna kill me, or they're not. God can worry about other shit with me."

"That's great if it gets you through the night, but I'd like to have the Almighty on my side going into combat."

"You don't think asking God to help you kill your fellow man is a little ass-backwards?"

"I'm not asking him to help me kill *anyone*. I'm just asking for his help in getting back home in one piece."

"In that case, say a prayer for both us, then. I don't feel like dying on the first trip out."

Tyler began to pray aloud. "Dear God, please bless this squadron, and protect our pilots and the innocent people on the ground. Please help our enemy see the errors of their ways and bring this horrible war to an end. Deliver the world and our country from the evils that have run rampant in recent times. Amen."

"Amen," Thomas replied. It was as close as he'd gotten to prayer in as long as he could remember.

Morning came hard and fast, and, after a quick breakfast, the boys headed to the hangars for what was supposed to be a routine mission. If all went as planned, they'd get a look at the scenic French coastline and be back in England in time for lunch.

"You ready for this?" Thomas asked Tyler as they got in their planes ahead of the takeoff signal.

"I'm scared shitless," Tyler replied, as his first-time nerves hadn't dissipated yet.

"I thought you chatted with the good Lord last night and He's gonna deliver us from evil," Thomas said.

"If he was ever gonna deliver me from evil, he'd send me to another unit, away from your act."

"Fair enough," Thomas said as he got in the plane and took off south toward Hitler's Fortressed Europe.

The English Channel looked calm and beautiful—in different circumstances, Thomas could see himself on a boat fishing for cod in the Channel, like he did for tuna off San Diego. The tranquility of the English Channel quickly gave way to a rocky coastline that served as the barrier between Hitler's reign of terror and the countless British, American, Free French, Polish, Czech and countless other nationalities building up in the U.K. who looked to defeat him. They flew over Le Havre, on the mouth of the Seine, which flows all the way to Paris. It was the perfect hiding spot for U-Boats and other German Navy crafts. The river served as a polluted vein in the body that was occupied France. Its mouth was only a hundred miles from Western Europe's last bastion of freedom—Great Britain—which sat guarded by countless allied soldiers who were willing to spill blood to keep the Isles free and were chomping at the bit to bring that very freedom back to rest of Europe.

"Holy Hell," Thomas said to himself as he saw the bombers drop their payloads on the piers and surrounding areas of Le Havre. He had seen plenty of wildfires in California, but this destruction was like nothing he had ever seen.

"So much for an easy mission," said a voice—Thomas assumed was Lieutenant Edelman—over the radio, as a pair of German fighters flying below the formation came into view.

Tyler's plane was the closest to the lead fighter, so he lowered his altitude, readied his machine gun and fired at the Messerschmitt fighter, *really* getting his combat cherry popped. Thomas meanwhile stayed in formation a few hundred yards away and watched his buddy fire at the German plane.

"I've got you, you son of a bitch," Lieutenant Donovan said as he again used his ever decreasing altitude to his advantage and swooped in on the enemy plane.

The German pilot never had a chance, as in attempting to ascend he made a mistake in turning his plane and turned himself into a sitting duck. Lieutenant Donovan's maneuver blew him right out of the sky. There was no time celebrate as there was another bandit on his tail that had gained altitude and snuck behind the American fighters while Tyler was engaged with his wingman.

"Decrease altitude, Ty," Thomas radioed as more of a suggestion than an order.

"Are you fucking serious? Do you want me to die?" Tyler replied as if he was flying any lower he'd be in some French fisherman's living room.

"Just do it! I know what I'm doing," Thomas said as he picked up speed and headed toward the lone enemy fighter. This was his first combat mission, so experience may not have been on his side, but his confidence and training were both there, and that meant something.

"You better not fuck this up, rookie," Lieutenant Gorman said over the radio, sure he was about to see his two newest squadron-mates die a horrific death on their first time out.

Lieutenant Donovan was dodging machine gun fire and was running out of options. "This better work," he said as he decreased altitude and made himself an even bigger target for his German counterpart.

Right on cue, Thomas opened fire as Tyler's plane was now out of the way and he was on a near-collision course with the bogie. The German pilot was late to go into a dive and pursued Tyler's plane as he was likely in shock that an enemy would make himself so vulnerable on urpose. That gave Thomas just the window he needed. As his bullets tore apart the German ighter, Thomas pulled up and regained altitude *just* before colliding with his enemy. It was a langerous game of chicken, and Thomas was loving every heart-pounding second. The damage vas done; the Messerschmitt was quickly losing altitude and eventually crashed into the drink.

"I hope they teach swimming lessons in Germany," Thomas radioed with a laugh.

"Don't let this go to your head, but you're alright, Whitney," Tyler said, knowing Thomas's unconventional maneuver, in all likelihood, had saved his life.

"Me, let something boost my ego? Never!" Thomas said, feeling pretty damn good about himself.

"Nice shooting, boys. The bombers have hit their targets. Time to go home," Major Leney radioed across the formation in a more casual manner than most of the veteran pilots were used to.

The return flight was smooth and silent, as neither the fighters nor the bombers lost a single pilot and the objectives were complete. Something about the flight back from a successful mission over occupied Europe gave the men of the squadron a sense of accomplishment mixed with a sense of longing. They had done a fantastic job, and, at least for the moment, the German war machine was weakened, but Europe still belonged to Hitler. They were thousands of feet in the air over a continent that was fortressed on the outside and run by an oppressive madman on the inside. The people of Europe needed to be freed, and the sooner, the better. But the higher-ups in London and Washington were no closer to establishing a date for a cross-Channel invasion than they were to discovering the lost city of Atlantis. For now, the pilots would have to keep doing their jobs, and their tiny planes would serve as little vehicles of freedom high above an enslaved people. As the squadron landed intact, the politics and specifics that had been on their minds gave way to graciousness as they got back on free British soil.

"So that's what it feels like to be in combat?" Thomas asked Lieutenant Gorman as they left their planes and headed toward Major Leney's office for debriefing.

"Yeah. You and your boy did well out there today. I'd tell you to try not to be a hero every time, but you've got balls, and I wouldn't want to castrate you," Lieutenant Gorman answered as he walked away.

Being validated like that from someone who had been in harm's way for a while gave Thomas a real sense of pride. He was high on himself for his efforts. Of course, he never lacked self-confidence, but this win was unique, and he truly savored it. Of course, this didn't stop him

"You know who I'm jealous of?" he asked Tyler as they headed toward the mess hall.

"Can't wait for this one," Tyler said, rolling his eyes.

"Bomber pilots. All they have to do is get over a target and drop their payload. That's it. We have to be glorified security and watch their sixes. If the Luftwaffe shows up, we have to be the ones to stand guard and take them on. If we don't do our jobs, they're as good as dead. If they don't do their jobs, then nothing happens. Think about it."

Tyler had grown into his role as the foil of his idealistic comrade and couldn't help but laugh. "Their job is to soften up Europe for the eventual invasion, and we have to be the guys who make sure they're safe while they're doing it."

"They still have it easier than us," Thomas said crassly. He didn't want his displeasure with how bombing runs were coordinated to become a debate on policy.

"Let's get some food—at least it'll give your mouth something to do other than gripe," Tyler said as they entered the mess hall.

"Like that's ever stopped me," Thomas answered, knowing damn well it would take far more than a sandwich for his opinions to be silenced.

September 10, 1943

Honington, England

Tyler and Thomas weren't green pilots anymore. They'd flown nearly a dozen combat missions and had earned the respect and admiration of their comrades. Major Leney had even lightened up a bit and allowed the pilots to paint subtle personal emblems and insignias on their planes, and Thomas couldn't help but notice the artwork on Tyler's as he walked toward the runway. He could see a massive Irish clover on the front of the plane and was intrigued by the writing that went with it.

"'Fighting Irish.' Let's hope our esteemed colleagues in the RAF don't see it—they might shoot you down before the Huns have a chance," Thomas said, looking over Tyler's paint job.

"While you're busy trying to piss of the Soviets, I can get on the shit list of the limeys. God knows they deserve it for what they've done to my people," Tyler replied. "My family was forced out of Ireland in the 1900s, and Union Jack soldiers were a big reason why."

"I'm sure Winnie Churchill himself will be shaking in his extra-large trousers when he sees the logo of a second-rate college football team darting through the sky."

"Someone's a little jealous of my artwork, aren't they?"

"You're a regular Van Gogh."

"What are you two ladies bitching at each other about now?" yelled Major Leney.

"College football, sir!" Tyler answered as he put his paintbrush down and saluted.

"Very good. I'd like a word with Lieutenant Whitney," the West Point graduate said as he took a few steps away from the runway.

"Yes, sir," Thomas began, "I feel like I'm being called to the principal's office." The young flyboy had been on Leney's shit list since day one and had gained a bit of a reputation around the base as being far from the perfect representative for the U.S. Army (bar room antics will do that), but his record in the air was astonishing.

"That's because you *are* being called to the principal's office. I want to start by saying you're one of the most self-involved, sarcastic, and at times reckless men I've ever served with. You are the exact opposite of what the Army looks for in an officer. Your day one antics and overall behavior since then would have had you thrown out of West Point before the first football game."

"You called me aside just to tell me that?" Thomas asked, really driving his commanding officer's point home and personifying the negative qualities that had just been listed.

"No, because despite that, you've also got balls of steel—you show zero fear in the sky, and when it's time to stand and deliver, there are few—if any—pilots I'd rather be flying with over hostile skies," said Leney. "You're loved and respected by the rest of the boys in the squadron, too—they see through your obnoxious exterior into the warrior soul inside. You guys could die on any one of these raids, but you're the one who keeps the mood loose, and that's more important than even you realize. I'm not sure how exactly you're wired or what your reason for being the way you are is, but this war will be won by men like you. Wars aren't won with armies of choir boys who have no flaws or thoughts of their own; they're won by the so-called bad boys, whose recklessness is only matched by their courage. Men who personify the fine line between careless and fearless and don't just preach the rebel spirit of our great country, but live it every day. I just thought you should know that. As you were." Major Leney turned and continued into his headquarters to plot out yet another mission somewhere over Germany.

For once in his life, Thomas Whitney was speechless. There was no wiseass remark or snarky retort he could make to the major, and as he got just outside of range, all Thomas could muster up was a simple, "Thank you, sir." His well-known negative characteristics were laid out in front of him, but Leney reminded him he had positive qualities. He was glad the major was willing to take the good with the bad. In a daze, he walked back to Tyler, who was deeply intent on his paint job.

"What did the major have to say?" Tyler asked.

"Shit about the war, obviously," Thomas said, as he shocked even himself by not bragging about the compliments he'd just gotten from his superior. "Speaking of shit, that artwork really is horrendous."

"I don't see you painting a soldier of Troy on your plane."

"I only paint confirmed kills on the side of my plane, and I've been busier than you since we got here," Thomas finished reminding Tyler that he had four confirmed kills, while Tyler still had just one from their first mission.

"We'll see who has the higher score when the war's over. You were an athlete, you know the only score that counts is the final one."

"You're right—the loser picks up the tab for the first post-war night of drinking, though," Thomas said as he headed away from the runway.

"Thank God your parents are rich, because I plan on running up one hell of a tab," Tyler said as Thomas was almost out of earshot. He could only shake his head at his more tame friend returning fire at him.

"You want to play some poker tonight?"

"Much as I would love to spend time with you and Brady, the thought of losing my hard-earned hazard pay to one of you degenerates isn't on the top of my list. They're playing a movie—I'd rather watch that and call it an early night."

"Suit yourself," Thomas said as he headed inside.

One of the perks—and stresses—of being a pilot was the slightly more prevalent downtime that existed for aviators, more so than in other branches of the service. Whitney's favorite activity during this downtime was playing poker with Lieutenant Ben Brady, an Albuquerque native who was as good on the shooting range as he was in the sky. Prior to joining the military, Brady was a courier pilot who had logged countless miles over the still somewhat wild American frontier. Unlike Thomas and Tyler, Brady was no spring chicken. He was over thirty when the war broke out, but his age was no hindrance, as his experience and dedication to duty were second to none. He and Thomas hit it off because he had Thomas's wild side and loved to have a good time when it was time to relax.

"When I walk into these barracks, I can't tell if I'm in Las Vegas or in dreary Britain," Thomas said as he walked toward Ben Brady's bunk.

"It sounds to me like you're looking to lose some money yet again," Lieutenant Brady said, putting his book down and breaking out a deck of cards.

"How's a 50 buck buy-in sound?"

"If you want to lose a week's pay, I'll be happy to take care of your money," the surly New Mexican said. He'd been on a bit of a winning streak against his fellow pilot.

The cards were dealt, and they both did their best to bluff the other one out of their money. By the time the final cards had been dealt, there was a massive pile of cash and trinkets on the bed in front of them. Thomas took one look at his hand—three kings smiled back—confidently smirked, and knew he was about to leave this game a richer man.

"I'm all in." Thomas grinned.

"How high do you want these stakes to go?"

"High as you want to go," Thomas said as he reached in his pocket, pulled out his Rose Bowl ring, and put it in the middle of the pile.

"A Rose Bowl championship ring?" balked Brady, looking at the ring, then at Thomas.

"You must feel pretty good about your chances." Lieutenant Brady—who had a pair of queens— felt his partner was bluffing and reached into his foot locker and pulled out a beautiful old west six-shooter that looked like something from a John Wayne movie. "My dad was a cavalry officer and made a bit of a name for himself on the frontier hunting Indians once upon a time. This was his sidearm, so if you've got the balls to put your Rose Bowl ring on the table, then hot damn, do I have the balls to put this in the pile."

Thomas almost felt guilty about taking such a prized possession from his friend, but they were gamblers, and they knew the rules when they showed up to the party. "We three kings of Thomas's hand are stealing revolvers!" Thomas sang as he laid his cards on the table.

"I haven't been this disappointed in a set of queens since I last saw my two ex-wives," Brady said as he handed over the pearl-handled revolver.

"I'll give you a chance to win it back sometime, but not today," Thomas said as he aimed the pistol down the empty barracks in a way that would make Wyatt Earp happy.

"I'm sure I'll win it back, but take care of the old girl in the meantime," Brady said like he was a parent dropping a child off at daycare.

"How does she shoot?"

"She's got some power; no aim, though, so Lord only knows where that bullet is going once you pull the trigger."

"Sounds like my kinda gal."

"Treat her right, because she's on loan to you until I can win her back."

"I may never lose again—this could be the start of a winning streak that would make the damn New York Yankees happy," Thomas said as he continued to play John Wayne with his new high-powered toy.

"You're no Joltin' Joe DiMaggio, in looks or talent," Ben said to bring his ever-cocky poker partner back to Earth.

"How convinced are we that WOP is even on our side? I hear FDR had his parents labeled as Mussolini's fellow travelers," Thomas said. He'd read that DiMaggio's Italian heritage got his parents put on an FBI watch-list.

"Gotta love this country. Joe leaves the Yanks to serve in the military, and his parents get branded enemies of the state," Ben replied.

"The twisted fucking irony that comes with war," said Thomas. "One member of the family is willing to die for a country that says his family could be our enemy because their last name ends with a vowel."

***

French Countryside

October 16, 1943

0430 hours

Rebecca and Thomas came to a break in the woods just before sunrise. They found themselves overlooking one of the many wineries that dotted the French countryside. The French love their vino, and no war or occupation would get in the way of that. Even the Germans had taken a liking to French wine since taking over, deviating from their national beverage: beer.

"That's a vineyard right there. We should be able to move through it and get to the other side before the sun comes up," Rebecca said as she quickly surveyed the landscape and saw the multiple buildings around it. They were in all likelihood occupied, and as good as glass of chardonnay might sound, they weren't exactly on a tour.

"I've been to Napa—I know what a vineyard is," Thomas said as he moved toward the rows and rows of grapes.

"What's Napa?" Rebecca whispered. She was far from an expert on Golden State geography.

"It's like if Tuscany washed up on the Pacific Coast and annexed a county in California," Thomas replied.

"So, people speak Italian there?" Rebecca asked. The partial language barrier and Thomas's weird sense of humor meant she still didn't have a clue what this Napa thing was.

"After enough bottles of chardonnay, they sure as hell sound like it," Thomas replied without answering Rebecca's question.

At this point, she gave up on Thomas and really couldn't care less about a stretch of land in northern California. She was in no mood to bicker with him while they were moving through property that was anything but unoccupied.

Before re-entering the dense woods beyond the winery, they caught a glimpse of the road that ran parallel to their route. Even at this hour, there was activity as Nazi vehicles powered down the road, conducting Lord only knows what type of evil activity, but the woods gave them the cover they sought and allowed them to settle down for the day. They had covered a lot of ground overnight and needed to rest before beginning the home stretch.

"What kind of wine do you think that vineyard makes?" Rebecca asked as she slumped down onto the base of a large tree.

"Probably cheap stuff. My parents say French wine is too acidic—not as good as Italian, and certainly not as good as Californian," Thomas quipped. His upper-class upbringing shone through, even on the edge of a vineyard thousands of miles from his home.

Once again, Rebecca was unfazed by Thomas's non-answer. "I liked chardonnay with family dinners before all of this started. I could use a bottle of it now."

Thomas knelt down and assumed the first watch while thinking about what Rebecca had just said. No one could use a drink more than him right now, and while the thought of sneaking into one of the buildings in the vineyard and stealing a bottle of wine sounded great, the name of the game was survival. He had last put a drink to his lips less than seventy-two hours earlier, but it might as well have been a lifetime ago on a continent far away.

"I could use a helluva lot more than just a chardonnay right now," Thomas said as he watched Rebecca fall asleep and thought back to the tap on the shoulder that brought him from an officer's bar in England to a cold, wooded area in occupied France.

***

Eighth Air Force Headquarters, Britain

October 13, 1943

1600 hours

Thomas was sitting in the officer's lounge, sipping on slightly sweet English stout and enjoying a twenty-four-hour pass while thinking about home. "All I want is a piece of land with the sand and salt and the world's best smell, where the waves are always rideable," he remarked to himself as he imagined the west coast near San Diego, how it was probably still sunny and warm. England, on the other hand, was getting colder—and the nights longer—with each passing day. The rain and notorious fog brought with them a type of misery that would pull down even the most jovial of people. How anyone could live in a place like this was beyond Thomas's comprehension, but his job wasn't to analyze the citizens of Britain—it was to win the war and get home as quickly as possible. He thought suicide rates in dreary places like the U.K. and even in America's Pacific Northwest must be astronomically high, and as someone who spent the bulk of his life in a place where it was sunny and seventy-five all the time, Thomas could see why.

He was in the middle of fantasizing about the Pacific Coast when he got a tap on the shoulder. "Report to HQ immediately. You've got work to do tomorrow," the enlisted runner, whom he knew by face but not name, told him before exiting the makeshift lounge.

He stared at his glass, examining the dark-as-night beer in his pint glass. "Is nothing sacred anymore? Can't a guy have a pint in peace without being interrupted by this damn war?" he said to no one in particular before finishing his drink and making the ninety-second walk across the runway to the briefing room.

"Lieutenant Whitney. How nice of you to join us," Major Leney said as Thomas gazed around the full room and quickly realized he was the last pilot to show.

"Sir, I had a twenty-four-hour pass, just for the record," Thomas said as he took a seat and gazed at the map and chalkboard at the front of the room.

"Well, I'm not sure if you've heard, but we're at war right now. We need our best and brightest pilots slaying the huns, not drinking all the beer in the British Isles, and unfortunately for us, that includes you. Understood, Lieutenant?"

"Yes, sir."

"Now that we're all here, let's get down to business," Major Leney began. "We've got a pretty juicy opportunity, if I do say so myself. The Krauts have a ball-bearing factory near Schweinfurt in southern Germany, and our boys in the Flying Fortresses are going to bomb it back to the Stone Age. While they're busy getting all the glory for putting a marginal dent in German manufacturing, we'll be up there providing fighter support and ensuring those filthy sons of bitches in the Luftwaffe go nowhere near our bombers, because we know how bomber pilots get when they actually have to defend themselves. Given the limitations of our fuel tanks, we won't be escorting the bombers all the way to the target. We'll take off after them, they'll use the element of surprise, and we'll meet them in the air over France while they're on their way back from the run. The brass figures the Krauts will be caught off-guard, and we'll only have to help them on their flight back. Be ready for takeoff at zero-seven-thirty, and God willing, you'll all be home for dinner tomorrow night. Familiarize yourselves with the maps of the area, have a cup of coffee, and be ready to unleash holy hell on any German pilot unlucky enough to take a shot at our bombers. Am I clear?"

"Yes, sir," the squadron responded in unison as they all almost simultaneously got up and examined the mission's maps and documents.

"Way to make an entrance," Lieutenant Donovan said to Thomas as they looked over their route, which would take them over occupied France and through enough anti-aircraft weaponry to down every Allied plane in Europe.

"I thought the Nazis took breaks so esteemed Army officers could enjoy the fruits of their labor at the officer's hall," Thomas responded.

"Look on the bright side—instead of giving some nurse or WAC girl the worst ten seconds of her life, you can give a Kraut pilot the final ten seconds of *his* life."

"Hell, I might just fly this plane clear across Europe, crash into Red Square, and personally shove my lucky pistol up Joe Stalin's ass."

"I had no idea P-51s could cross an entire continent. You should tell Leney, maybe he'll let us go all the way to Germany. Besides, it's not like we need the Russian Army to help us beat Hitler or anything."

"We'll need the German Army to beat Stalin, so maybe I can be the guy that dies making that happen, sooner rather than later."

"Always have an answer, and it's rarely the right one," Lieutenant Donovan said as the two headed out the door and into the brisk British evening.

"When this is all said and done, you'll be happy to have served with such a worldly guy like me."

"Some lucky son of a bitch in the Marine Corps is serving with Ted Williams and gets to hear stories about winning the Triple Crown, and I'm stuck serving with Thomas 'Let's-go-to-war-with-Russia' Whitney."

"William is a bum. I struck—" Thomas attempted to recount his story, but Donovan interrupted him.

"I know, I know, you played against Teddy Ballgame and struck him out on three pitches during your junior year in high school. That's why *you're* on the payroll of the Boston Red Sox and *he* was working in a bar in Santa Monica when the Japs bombed Pearl Harbor."

"You know, there's a second part of that story I haven't told anyone since high school," Thomas replied, shaking off the criticism. There was no way that one of his proudest moments in life had become a redundant story that absolutely nobody wanted to hear any more.

"I can't wait to hear this bullshit," Tyler said as he rolled his eyes.

"Next at bat," Thomas began, all but ignoring the crass comments from his bunkmate, "Williams steps into the batter's box." He began mimicking the Splendid Splinter's signature left-handed stance. "First pitch, I throw a damn near perfect fastball on the outside corner that I thought would either graze the strike zone or, at worst, have ball one. Teddy got *all* of it and hit a ome run to centerfield that might as well have landed in Temecula. That was the day I knew for ertain baseball wasn't for me."

"And your life has been aces ever since."

"Shit. I won a Rose Bowl, met you, and get to be part of this whole thing. It's been an nteresting run to say the least," Thomas said as he held the door to the barracks open.

The two had a few laughs and played some cards—Tyler would always be up for a game f blackjack, but never bet the way Thomas and other members of the squadron did—before alling it a night early.

For all the teasing and shit-talking that went on between the two of them, they had a pecial bond that could only be fostered by the willingness to die for one another in combat. Jnlike when they first arrived in Europe, there was no all-night tossing and turning before nissions; it had become, in a way, almost routine. They had a job to do, and the stakes were iigh, but when their heads hit the pillows now, they were out for the count.

At breakfast the next morning, the fear of what they were about to do didn't hurt their ppetites—Thomas even went up for seconds, since there wasn't anywhere to get food at 30,000 eet over Europe. Even their discussions at the breakfast table were on anything but the mission t hand. Baseball—more specifically, the recently-completed World Series that saw the New York Yankees beat the St. Louis Cardinals—was on everyone's mind, and that took precedence ver the task at hand. America's pastime became a nice escape from the war, and the Army sent eels overseas so the soldiers and airmen could see highlights of the Fall Classic.

"Look on the bright side, Tyler—you got to see the team that won the World Series play his season," Thomas said, ribbing his Red Sox fan wingman, referring to a Yankees/Detroit Tigers game they'd attended while they were still in New York City.

"So, potentially, getting killed in combat wouldn't be the worst thing to happen to me this year," Donovan fired back.

The squadron wrapped up breakfast and made their way into their planes. Once again, ike clockwork, it was time to go to work.

"Don't pull any stupid shit up there," Thomas said almost sarcastically to his straight-laced wingman as they headed to the runway for what was sure to be one of their more memorable missions.

"I'll try not to *accidently* strafe you and deprive the U.S. Army of its most self-centered pilot."

"Good. I'll try not to kill every single German pilot."

"I like it—save some for the rest of us," Tyler said, Thomas's self-confidence never ceasing to amaze him. It was contagious, and Lieutenant Donovan always felt better flying into hostile skies with Thomas's bravado up there with him.

The two shook hands before getting in their planes and taking off over the British countryside.

Escorting this raid over southern Germany was going to be the longest the unit had undertaken and would really push the engines of the P-51s. They would be almost in a holding pattern over France while the bombers completed their mission. It also served as a reminder of just how much territory the Nazis occupied. These missions would soften up the targets behind enemy lines and help slow down German manufacturing of war materials. The long-range bombers were going to be a small part of the eventual liberation of Europe, and the fighters needed to ensure their job could be done uninterrupted and with surgical precision.

Looking down at the woods, farmland, and rail lines that dotted the French countryside, Thomas thought back to the last time he was here and how much had changed. He was now a mile above the railways that brought him across Europe in 1935, and his mission was to help liberate a world that seemed to be gone completely. With each bomb that landed on European soil, people, places, and landscapes were being destroyed or altered forever. The concept of liberation was, at least in his eyes, the polar opposite of what they were helping the bombers do, but it wasn't his job to make policy. All he knew was that a cross-Channel invasion better happen soon, or there wouldn't be a Europe to liberate—only the charred wreckage of a once-beautiful continent.

Much like their first raid over Le Havre, the fighters were there to a certain degree as spectators, watching the bombers level a number of German factories and military targets. This time, however, they knew they'd have company—and not the invited kind.

"Here come the Huns," Lieutenant Gorman said as a pack of roughly half a dozen Luftwaffe fighters came into view. The American squadron outnumbered their enemy counterparts—despite playing this game on the road, they had at least one major advantage.

"Copy that. Let's keep the bombers safe," Thomas radioed as he and the rest of the unit moved to engage the hostile aircraft.

The squadron stayed in formation and used their precision, training, and superior American machinery to take on their foes. Lieutenant Whitney barrel rolled from his altitude right into the German formation and blew one plane out of the sky-his fifth kill-securing his status as an ace. On the descent, he reversed an old trick, decreasing altitude to confuse the enemy and giving Lieutenant Donovan a clear lane to engage the befuddled German pilots head on.

This time around, it didn't work *as* perfectly. Whitney's plane took heavy fire and became a collection of bullet holes with some metal in between.

"What's your status, Whitney?" Major Leney radioed in.

"I'm hit bad, but I'm still flying. No quit, sir."

"Roger that, son," Leney sent across the formation. "The bombers are in bound, and we're heading home. We're not out of the woods yet, but good job, men."

Thomas's plane was still flying, but another few rounds of machine gun fire, and it'd be game over for his aircraft. Tyler's plane was in slightly better shape, but had taken some damage during the dogfight. The sky was clear of enemy planes, but he knew at any point, the Luftwaffe could scramble enough fighters to put him in an early grave. Sure enough, somewhere over the French/German frontier, a lone Me-109 came from Thomas's port side.

"We've got company at nine o'clock," Lieutenant Whitney radioed.

"Copy that. Let's turn him into a damn schnitzel," Donovan responded.

Thomas maneuvered his damaged plane to try to get some altitude, but before he could do that, the streaking German fighter opened fire and got a direct hit on his fuel tank. "Oh fuck, I'm going down," he radioed. He was losing altitude—and any hope of getting back to England. The German fighter disappeared into the sunlight for a hot second, but the pilots were sure it would be back with a vengeance to finish the job.

"Try to stabilize and put her down in a field—give yourself a puncher's chance," Leney said over the radio. They were over occupied France, and landing meant almost certain capture.

"No shit, Sherlock," Thomas replied. "Someone get this son of a bitch off my ass. and I'l write from the POW camp, sir."

Thomas wasn't finished speaking when the pesky fighter came back with a roaring fury, hell bent on adding another kill to his resume. This time, it went hard after Lieutenant Donovan's plane.

"Time to play some chicken with this little fuck," Tyler proclaimed as smoke began billowing from his wing following a direct hit.

The more smoke he saw, the more he realized he, like Thomas, wouldn't be making it back to England in one piece. Rather than bail out or go down with the plane, he had a better idea: take this sorry excuse for a fighter pilot down with him and give his friend a chance to survive. "Godspeed, gentlemen. I've got this guy," he screamed as he squeezed the machine gun trigger and sped right toward his German counterpart.

"Have you lost your fucking mind?!" Thomas screamed into his headset, knowing his friend had, in no uncertain terms, committed a suicide maneuver in hopes of downing the enemy plane and giving him a chance to at least put the plane down.

"No more than you have. Go, Irish!" was the last radio message from Tyler's plane before the midair collision happened and both planes were incinerated on impact. Given his dropping altitude, Thomas didn't have the best view of the collision, but he heard the explosion and caught sight of some of the debris falling to the ground in the reflection from his cockpit.

Despite trying otherwise, all Thomas wanted to do was cry. His best friend had just laid down his life to give him a chance at survival, and that was the sort of emotional shot in the gut hat human emotions just weren't prepared for. There was no time to cry right now; he was osing altitude, and, fortunately for him, a wide open field appeared on the horizon. Thomas vasn't a fan of parachutes by any means; he'd rather put the plane down himself like a glider, so ailing out was completely off the table.

There was no way to tell where he was in the French frontier, nor where or how many German troops were nearby, but those bridges could be crossed if and when he survived the rash. He readied his plane for impact and tried to land softly on what he assumed was an uneven urface. As he turned the engine off and let the plane glide toward the earth, he saw farmhouses nd woods, both of which could be either advantageous or death traps depending on how many German troops were in the area. The plane violently landed wheels first and glided as Thomas ad made it more of a crash landing than a crash and burn. When the plane finally came to a omplete stop, he caught his breath and realized it was time to move out. The landing surely ttracted some attention, and that was the last thing he needed. He ditched his jacket and nything that could weigh him down and grabbed only the essentials—his government-issue istol, the lucky and loaded six-shooter, two chocolate bars, his compass, a flashlight, and a pair f maps.

It was broad daylight, so once he got out of the downed aircraft, he broke for the wooded rea that was about half a football field away from the crash site. If he was wounded in the crash, e wasn't feeling it; adrenaline had completely taken over. He sprinted across the field into the voods like he was still on the kickoff unit for the Trojans. He didn't stop running when he got nto the wooded area, but he slowed down and tried to find a place where he could examine the naps and try to figure out just where the hell he was.

He sprinted for what he figured was seven minutes through the woods of France before topping. If Nazi troops were looking for him—surely, they were—they weren't exactly hot on is trail at the moment, and that gave him time to figure out where he was and what the next step vould be. Laying out the old Army-issue map of France, Germany, and Switzerland and etracing his flight route after the bombing, he deduced he was somewhere near Besançon, which neant the Swiss border was to the East. Switzerland was a neutral country—free from the arnage that had engulfed the rest of the continent—and it gave him at least a chance of rejoining he war effort. He still wasn't completely sure where he was, but he took one last look at the map before beginning to move due east, according to his compass. He knew by now the Germans had gotten to his crash site and were looking for yet another American aviator for their POW camps. While maneuvering through the woods, he kept his ears peeled for any other sounds of movement. Something so slight as the snap of a twig was enough reason to freeze and take cover. *This is just like the time in high school I took Jenny Cole home when my parents were upstairs*, he thought to himself.

For a few hours, he wandered through the woods until he came across a stream to rehydrate and wash some of the sweat from his face. The stream appeared to be flowing southwest, so following it to the source, likely in the mountains of Switzerland, seemed like a slightly better approach than wandering aimlessly through the woods of Europe. About a mile down the path, he saw a small footbridge over the stream with two German soldiers standing guard—one on both ends.

"Fuck. Guests at the party, yet again," he whispered as he ducked down to avoid being detected. He knew they couldn't be the only patrols in the area, and it wasn't unreasonable to assume they had heard about a downed aircraft and an Allied pilot on the run. Rather than try to sneak by the sentries during the day, Thomas decided to wait them out and try to advance past the bridge when the sun went down. Luckily for Thomas, there was a patch of bushes along the banks of the stream that gave him optimal cover until the time was right.

The two German soldiers stayed mostly stationary for hours, only moving to switch positions and stretch their legs. By the time night time had come, the duo at the bridge had been relieved by a pair of fresh sentries who would be pulling the graveyard shift. At some point during the night, he noticed one sentry walk into the woods to relieve himself—now was the time to move. Under cover of darkness and moving slowly enough to have the flowing stream mask his steps, he moved toward the bridge and ducked under the bridge itself, positioning his backside on the bank and his boots in the water.

"Now what?" he thought to himself as he realized he was now directly under two enemy soldiers, both literally and figuratively cornered.

***

Roughly 40 miles from the Swiss Border

October 16, 1943

1030 hours

Thomas and Rebecca settled in for their second day of sitting tight, trying to get sleep and hoping like hell that the German Army was patrolling another patch of the French countryside. Neither one found these accommodations—the base of a large pine tree—luxurious either, but once again, it beat being in captivity.

With both of them wide awake on this very brisk fall morning, Thomas—as he had always done—spoke his mind. "I don't understand how the continent of Europe could have let things get this bad this fast. Did anyone have the balls to stand up to Hitler before he felt the need to conquer a continent?"

"I beg your pardon?" a very groggy Rebecca asked. She was still unsure what Thomas's point was or why it warranted this outburst in the midst of their hiding out.

"If the countries of Western Europe weren't going to stop Hitler, they might as well have joined and wiped those the Bolsheviks in Russia off the map. Ridding the world of the stain that is communism is quite the noble deed if you ask me," Thomas said, as the sleep deprivation and hunger had gotten to him, making his opinions more obnoxious and somehow even less sensible.

By this point, Rebecca had had it. She used what little energy she had and jumped to her feet. She was not going to be lectured on European politics by some Yankee who put his never-ending idealism ahead of her actual experience. "You're from a country on the other side of a vast ocean, and you speak about European politics and affairs like you're well-versed. What gives you the right to tell Europeans how to conduct their business?"

Thomas didn't want to get into a screaming match with the ever-likely possibility of German patrols possibly anywhere, but he had a point to get across. "Hey, I saw firsthand how evil Stalin was when I was in Russia as a kid. I haven't lived my whole life in a domestic bubble like so many other G.I.s."

"You *saw* how evil Stalin was firsthand? Congratulations, I *lived* through the terror that was Hitler after the invasion, and if we don't get out of here, we'll really see just how bad the fascists can be."

All Thomas could do was stand there like a statue. She had him beat, and ending up in a POW camp to see just how bad the Nazis treated prisoners wasn't how he wanted to find out whether Hitler was worse than Stalin. Even still, that trip to Russia almost a decade earlier came back to him. Unlike countless American servicemen in World War II who saw the world through the lens of the Great Depression, Thomas had seen plenty of the world *before* he shipped out. He sat down, shut up, and thought back to his last real taste of innocence.

***

Union of Soviet Socialist Republics

July 10, 1935

After three years of starring on the varsity football team at Oceanside High School outside San Diego, Thomas would spend his senior year of high school and football at Deerfield Academy in Massachusetts, as his father, uncle, and grandfather had before him. Moving nearly 3,000 miles for a year of high school might seem insane to some, but to the Whitney family, it was a tradition worth keeping, regardless of the distance. By now, Thomas's exploits on the gridiron had earned him scholarship offers from powerhouse west coast programs such as USC and UCLA, but in order to matriculate at such prestigious institutions, he'd need better grades than he was getting at his California public high school. In the summer of 1935, before he began at Deerfield, the family traveled half a world away to visit Thomas's Uncle Craig and his family, who was working for the newly-reopened U.S. Embassy in Moscow.

The journey from San Diego to the Soviet capital took almost three weeks. A trans-Pacific freighter took them from the coast of California to Tokyo in eleven days. It was no luxury liner, but given it was made by Whitney Shipbuilders, the family had very good accommodations for the voyage across the world's largest ocean. The ship the family was traveling in was built for speed as well as raw power. It could shave a full day off a trans-Pacific voyage, which made all the difference in the world for travelers

The family spent a night in Tokyo before taking a ferry from Japan to Vladivostok and riding the Trans-Siberian Railway to Moscow in a solid ten days. The elder Whitneys wanted to use this adventure as an opportunity to travel around the world; they planned to leave Russia by train and travel west through Europe by passenger ship from Antwerp to Boston. They'd drop Thomas off at Deerfield, then go back to California from there. It would be slightly more luxurious than the one Ferdinand Magellan took many centuries earlier.

By day nineteen, a now very antsy teenage Thomas was growing frustrated. "How much longer?" he asked as he looked out the window of the passenger car that was rolling through the Ural Mountains, not far from where the Romanovs, the ruling family of Russia for centuries, were murdered by the brutal Bolshevik government that ruled the renamed Union of Soviet Socialist Republics.

Putting down *A Farewell to Arms*, Ernest Hemingway's latest work, for the first time in hours, Matthew looked over at his son. "We'll be in Moscow tomorrow night."

"Thank God. I've seen more of the world through the window of a ship and train than I ever want to again."

"You're acting ungrateful," Katlyn chimed in to bring her son back down to earth. "Most of America is living in poverty, but you get to travel the world." With age came perspective, but the Irish in her had no issue expediting that process. "You'll get to see your cousin Brian tonight, and I'm sure you boys will hit it off once again."

"You're right," Thomas said, realizing it had been a while since he and Brian had seen each other. Brian was only a year younger than him, and while Brian grew up all over the country—his father's job required much travel—the duo always seemed to pick up right where they had left off. "I just wish these Soviets were as good at making comfortable seats on trains as they are at murdering their own people."

This outburst from a loud-mouthed seventeen-year-old drew the ire of Matthew, who sprung toward his son, grabbed him by the collar, and forcefully whispered in his ear. "Listen, and listen to me good: we're not in America anymore. There's no freedom of speech, so keep your fucking mouth shut. You don't know who's listening. Just keep quiet, and spew all the venom you want when we get back stateside next month. Do you understand?"

"Yes, sir," Thomas answered, as he went back to staring aimlessly into the Russian frontier and watching tiny village after tiny village pass by.

"Good. Now let's try to get to Moscow without starting an international incident, shall we?" Matthew reached for his Hemingway novel.

"I just wish flying was an option, we'd save so much time if we could have just flown from California," Thomas said in a way only a teenager ever could.

"Well, learn to fly an airplane, and you can get yourself across the world at a speed that works for you," Katlyn said as she attempted to nap in her seat.

"Maybe I will," Thomas answered, keeping his stare pointed out the somewhat cracked window of the swiftly moving train.

***

Moscow, Union of Soviet Socialist Republics

July 11, 1935

Upon arriving in Moscow, the family was whisked a short distance away by the U.S. Embassy's private car to the Dacha, where they were staying. Craig and his wife Maryalice's residence was on the same street, and sure enough, when the car turned the corner, the "other" Whitneys were waiting in front of their home to serve as a de facto welcoming committee. The car hadn't even come to a full and complete stop when the Whitney family poured out and began embracing their relatives.

"Been a while since you've been in this country," Craig said, referring to his brother's U.S. Army service on Russia's Pacific Coast in World War I. The two brothers embraced.

"Seventeen years since I left Vladivostok, courtesy of a bullet wound in my shoulder from a damn commie. Now those bastards are running this place, and the guy who shot me is probably best friends with Stalin."

"You were freezing your bag off in Vladdy and getting shot at while I was drinking cognac and wine in Paris on Armistice Day," Craig said as he joyfully recounted his days as an Army officer in France during the Great War.

"Life's imperfect."

The dacha the family was staying in on the outskirts of Moscow was not only beautiful, but less than 100 yards away from where Craig, Maryalice, and Brian had taken up residence. In an era before theme parks and all-inclusive resorts, the spot had one of the best amenities for traveling with a youngster—a swimming pool. As they examined their surroundings, they had one rude awakening: they would not be staying alone, as there was a guest unit at the back of their quarters that was clearly in use. As they walked toward the door, it sprung open, and a uniformed NKVD—Stalin's not-so-secret police—came out and greeted them.

"Captain Petya Folanov, I'll be here to make sure your stay in our country is an enjoyable one," he said in almost perfect English, masked by a thick Slavic accent.

"I don't understand," Matthew began. "We weren't told anything about having a supervisor on the property."

"We like to keep an eye on our foreign guests. Make sure you enjoy your time here and ensure you don't do anything to undermine our great socialist society."

Before Thomas could say a word to the spectacled Russian, Katlyn put her hand over his mouth. The teen thought he was wise beyond his years, and his attitude ran opposite to the then-contemporary ideal that children were to be seen and not heard.

"So, we're being babysat like a group of criminals," Matthew said. He knew Soviet Russia was screwed up, but this was just bizarre.

"We just want to make sure your stay is a pleasant one for yourself and for our great country."

"This shit is par for the course," Craig whispered to his brother as the Russian stood before them. "I thought you knew that."

"No, I missed that memo, but I guess we can live with it."

Thomas looked on, disappointed, knowing his family would be under constant watch from this Russian servant of Stalin, but he for once in his life stayed silent, mainly because his mother's hand was still covering his mouth.

"Excellent. Now enjoy your stay in the Union of Soviet Socialist Republics," Folanov said as he retreated into the guest house.

"Do all foreigners get babysat like this?" Thomas asked, breaking his silence once the Russian was out of earshot.

"Pretty much," Craig replied honestly to his nephew. "We don't have one living on the premises, but God knows they're around at all times. You just can't see them."

In honor of the family's first night in Russia, Craig and Maryalice prepared a feast for their guests and made the dacha feel as much like home as possible. Settling into the multicourse meal of caviar, golubtsy, pelmeri, and countless other local dishes, it was time to get caught up on family and world business, as the two went hand in hand for the Whitneys.

"How are things Stateside?" Craig asked, even though it had been less than three months since his family moved to Russia.

"The economy still sucks, but according to everyone, Roosevelt is gonna save us all. I'll believe it when I see it."

"Hey, Franklin got me this job, so he's not all bad."

"One Harvard man taking care of another," replied Matthew. "A tradition as old as time itself."

"Don't be jealous you didn't get into Harvard and had to *settle* for Stanford," Craig said to his brother as though there was something wrong with going to the most esteemed university in Northern California.

"I can't wait to *not* vote for Roosevelt next November. One term is enough."

"I still don't get why you hate him so much."

"He's a damn communist—really no better than Josef Stalin here," Matthew said in a sentence that belonged in the Hyperbole Hall of Fame.

"I'll make sure to tell him to take you off the Christmas card list this year," Craig playfully said.

"He didn't do shit to pass the anti-lynching bill a few years ago," said Matthew, referring to FDR's unwillingness to make racial based lynchings a federal crime in 1933. "The man is a damn racist—our father always treated the colored folks well and created jobs for men from all walks of life. I don't think the president sees things that way."

"Dad was always right about that. Doesn't matter the color of a man's skin, only the work he puts in every day," Craig said, thinking back to the way their father saw through skin color to get the most out of workers every day—even if it was only to maintain a healthy bottom line on his own end.

"He was a great man, unlike the fuck that's running this country. I tell you, the damn commies never should've greased the Czar and his ministers," Matthew said.

"You might want to keep it down—we don't know what's bugged and what isn't," replied Craig. "Even if Folanov isn't in the room, he likely knows what's going on. If you do want to talk about dangerous racism, that guy in Berlin scares the hell out of me. He's crazy enough to bring another continent-wide war."

"That Austrian corporal!?" blurted Matthew. "He's got the country back up and running—and militarized again, to boot. Do you really think he'd want a repeat, though?"

"I do think he's crazy enough to have another Great War if it means re-establishing Germany as a superpower," Craig supposed. "Time will tell if anyone else steps up and puts him in his place, but if he goes unchecked, I shudder at the thought of what the world will look like."

Thomas and Brian sat and listened, and like most youngsters, took in their parents' ideas like sponges. They weren't too young to form their own views anymore, but it went without saying that the at-times contrarian views of their fathers shaped their own worldviews.

"We'll see," said Craig, then turned to Thomas, looking to change the subject to something lighter. "So, Thomas, I hear it's off to Deerfield then to a big-time football school for you. Anywhere specific in mind?" His nephew's exploits on the gridiron offered the perfect escape from the world gone mad around him.

"Yes, Uncle Craig. I'm hoping either Michigan or the University of Southern California."

"Good man—both programs are excellent. Brian is looking at West Point on an academic scholarship—he wants to be an officer in the Army."

"Here's to our two successful boys," Katlyn said as she raised her glass of Georgian wine for a toast, and the rest of the dinner party followed suit—even the boys raised up their glasses of far-from-pure Russian water.

"I'll never understand these women that have a dozen or so children. It's about the quality, not quantity, of your spawn that makes a difference," Maryalice said to Katlyn as soon as she finished her toast. The two families had only one son each, but both mothers thought they were as handsome as they were smart and would surely have the world by the proverbial balls in the years to follow.

After dinner, while their fathers smoked cigars and made a dent in Craig's expansive brandy collection and their mothers sat in the parlor and talked about their husbands and sons, the boys had a catch with a baseball and a pair of gloves by the swimming pool and enjoyed the balmy Moscow summer night. The trip may have taken forever, but Thomas didn't forget to pack a football, as he was almost positive the sporting goods stores of Moscow wouldn't carry them. Of course, all of this went on under the watchful eye of the ruthless Captain Folanov.

"How do you go to school out here?" Thomas asked his cousin as they threw the ball back and forth.

"We have an American school at the embassy. I'm out for the summer right now, though."

"Any girls?" Thomas asked, addressing the subject on the mind of seemingly every teenaged boy everywhere.

"Some. The Russian girls that live right near the embassy are so beautiful. I really wish we were allowed to talk to them. I speak Russian, you know."

"Why can't you talk to them?"

"The government here doesn't like foreigners, and if they see us talking to them, we can both get in big trouble."

Growing up with a silver spoon in his mouth in San Diego, Thomas's idea of trouble was a far cry from his cousin's experience in an oppressive dictatorship, but even still, Thomas had to make a comment. "Buddy, I sneak beers into Pacific Beach when I go surfing—I know trouble. Let's get in some trouble while I'm here."

"Well, the NKVD is a lot less forgiving than the San Diego Police Department. There's no due process over here. They are judge, jury, and executioner."

"Sounds like the perfect group to introduce myself to," Thomas said. It didn't matter where he was or how bad the people he wasn't supposed to piss off were, he was Thomas Whitney, and that was that.

The two boys walked down the streets, keeping their American paperwork on them at all times. Thomas saw her in a café—one of the most beautiful women he had ever laid his eyes on—reading a Tolstoy novel. Every stereotype about Russian women being ugly went right out the window. Her blonde hair's divine beauty was matched only by the bluest eyes he had ever seen—the kind of eyes that would bring even the baddest guy to his knees.

"Holy hell, is she pretty," Thomas said to Brian as they walked closer.

"She goes to the American school—her father does work for the Embassy. Her name is Anna, and she's actually really nice," Brian replied.

"Do you want to introduce me?"

"I told you—we can get in trouble if we talk to Russian girls out here."

"What are they gonna do to me again? I forget."

As much as Brian wanted to remind his more carefree cousin about the dangers of getting on the NKVD's bad side, he really didn't have concrete facts to back up his argument. He had heard plenty of rumors of people disappearing, but no one he knew had disappeared, and he figured if he lied to Thomas, he'd still call his bluff. Before Brian could get over there to make the introductions, Thomas had already walked over to Russia's most beautiful ambassador and was already making an ass of himself on the international stage.

"Pry-vieta," Thomas said, completely butchering the Russian word for "hello" and playing the obnoxious American asshole to a tee.

While slightly startled at the somewhat aggressive greeting, the bombshell put her book down, smiled at the American, and replied, "I'm Anna. I go to the American school, so I speak English. You don't have to try to speak Russian and sound so foolish."

Thomas was humbled by the directness and bluntness of the Russian beauty, who spoke a purer form of English than most Americans, albeit with a slight Slavic accent. "Let me start over again. Hello, my name is Thomas."

"Nice to meet you," she replied and smiled. "I saw you come in with Brian. Do you know each other?"

"He's my cousin. I'm visiting from America."

"Well, welcome to Russia. Take a seat, and tell Brian to come over here, too. We never really get to talk outside of class."

Brian watched the introductions from a distance. He'd missed the specifics of the conversation, but just from their body language, he more than got the gist of it. Once Thomas waved him over, he smiled, shook his head, and took another seat at the table. The repercussions he'd heard about for fraternizing with Russian citizens were still front and center in Brian's mind, but Thomas's confidence, and Anna's at least somewhat warm welcome, alleviated his fears about what Stalin's maniacal reign of terror could bring on the youthful trio.

"Why don't you ever talk to me or any of the other Russians in class outside of school when we see each other?" Anna asked Brian, being overtly blunt once again.

Brian didn't know the best way to answer the question. Answering it honestly would highlight the mostly unspoken fears of almost everyone in Russia—that Stalin could and would kill anyone for any reason. Then again, almost any other answer would paint him as xenophobic. He never felt racially, ethnically, or culturally superior to his Russian peers, but he could see that his lack of any real communication with them outside the walls of the classroom painted that illusion.

"My parents keep me on a tight leash," he answered, leaving out key details while still telling the truth.

His sentence and euphemism was lost in translation as Anna started laughing. "They treat you like a dog?! Americans are weird."

Thomas joined in the laughter and chimed in while rubbing his cousin's head like a shih tzu. "He's a good boy."

"You came all this way just to visit?" Anna asked, as she couldn't wrap her mind around traveling across the world for just a few short weeks together as a family.

"Yes, we like to travel. Especially to family and friends. Brian is family, and I think now, you and I are friends," Thomas said in such a smooth manner that even a world-renowned Casanova like Errol Flynn would've been proud.

Anna was impressed by the bravado of her American peer, but she wasn't exactly blown away. Maybe in America, he'd wow any girl with his confidence and cherubic good looks, but this was a long way from the USA. "I have a lot of friends," she answered, "and now you're one of them."

"Fair enough," Thomas said as the international ice had been broken. Brian may have been afraid of the Russian government, but he wasn't. There was a gorgeous girl sitting across the table from him, and no dictator or demented form of government would get in the way. He looked across the table at Brian, who sat there silently, still somewhat nervous about the ongoing interaction. If Brian didn't have the testicular fortitude to try to woo a natural beauty like Anna, then it'd be his loss. Maybe he could learn a thing or two from watching the self-proclaimed teenaged master at work.

Somewhere between Besançon and the Swiss Border

October 16, 1943

2330 hours

The political discussions subsided, and over the course of the day, both Thomas and Rebecca were able to get some sleep and regain energy for what would be the final pushes toward freedom. They marched through the forests, knowing danger could be at any turn and that as little as crunching on a pine needle could alert a suspicious enemy soldier. The woods were getting thinner and thinner, and with each passing moment, daylight came closer. It didn't take a Rhodes scholar to know that a town was nearby, but which town and how close were the questions on the minds of both Thomas and Rebecca. Hopefully, there would be some sort of barrier between the woods and the town, since walking right into the center of an occupied town at this time of night was like sending a beacon to the Nazis and their collaborators within the French populous. Sure enough, there was a break in the woods *just* before the buildings of the town appeared, giving Thomas and Rebecca time to take cover and cautiously walk along the outskirts to better gain their bearings.

"Morteau," Rebecca whispered.

"Excuse me?"

"This is the town of Morteau," repeated Rebecca. "My cousins live here, or used to live here. We're less than forty kilometers from the border." Her description contained yet another sad personal note as to how this war had ripped apart her family.

"Two more nights?" Thomas said, thinking out loud about the time they'd have between now and reaching Switzerland.

"Yes, about that."

The cold air hit the California kid like a sledgehammer, and he did everything he could to avoid shivering too loudly. "At times like this, I wish I was stationed in the Philippines with my cousin Brian. At least it's warm out there all the time."

"What was your cousin's story?" Rebecca asked. In this circumstance, silence may have been golden, but this one was awkwardly deafening, and she sought to get to know her escape partner a little better.

"He ended up going to West Point, graduated in June of 1941, and was stationed in the Philippines under General MacArthur," Thomas whispered, still concerned about being found. "When they fell to the Japs, he went missing. We have no idea where he is right now. Could be dead, could be fighting as a guerilla, could be languishing in a prison." Thomas and his family had been pondering just what Brian's fate was after the Japanese conquest of the Philippines in 1942. He then thought back to the last time the two of them were together at the very end of his family's fateful trip to Moscow.

***

Moscow, Union of Soviet Socialist Republics

August 1, 1935

There was a big to-do in the Kremlin as the ambassadors of several countries—the US, the UK, France, and Nazi Germany, specifically—their families and other foreign dignitaries were to be personal guests of the Secretary of the Communist Party, Joseph Stalin. For some reason, the Communist Party of the Soviet Union wanted to show off what the motherland could offer its foreign guests, and no expense was spared by the Kremlin. Except for the two American teenagers, it was an adults-only event that featured countless platters of Soviet dishes, and all the vodka, brandy, and wine from the Caucasus Mountains that Russians and Westerners could ever desire. The festivities also coincided with Matthew, Katlyn, and Thomas's last night in the country, so, in essence, it worked as a going away party for their side of the family.

"We need a nickname for Stalin," Thomas said, as he squinted to make out the dictator sitting up front at the head table. If the Whitneys were any further back, they'd be at the dreaded "kid's table" at any American house on Thanksgiving.

"The Red Murderer," Brian answered in a quiet voice.

"How about Corrupt Dwarf?" Thomas fired back slightly louder, as he left any fear of consequences at the door.

"That works, too."

"Boys, be polite—we're guests in his country right now," Katlyn said, since causing an international incident because her son and nephew were unfiltered wasn't exactly what she had in mind as their trip to Russia wound down.

The energetic duo immediately went silent. The rest of the world may have been up for debate, but Mom laying down a proclamation was an absolute certainty and not up for discussion. Russian leader was a short and stubby man, but his presence was felt by all. He may not have been handsome, tall, or fit, but he had the power to kill or imprison anyone he chose, and that power and voracity outweighed any physical appearance. As the meal was served,

Thomas kept his eye on the front of the room. He had developed a weird fascination with being in the same room as Stalin.

"May I be excused to use the restroom?" Thomas asked.

"Of course. I believe it's back there on the left," Matthew said as he took another sip of vodka on the rocks—no mixer, of course.

Thomas navigated the crowd and found the tiny restroom that was a far cry from ones he had seen in the Western world. As he walked out of the bathroom, he turned and saw Premier Stalin. The short and stumpy murderer looked more like a peasant that should be tilling a plot of land outside of St. Petersburg than a world leader. He was accompanied by two bodyguards who had alpha-male written all over them. They gave the impression that no one was to so much as glare at the Premier the wrong way. Thomas was feeling a little adventurous and wanted to make his opinion known to the Soviet leader.

"Hey, Joe," he shouted, causing Stalin and his mini-entourage to turn around. "You're an asshole. Translate that."

Stalin's translator, who was clearly a hall of fame 'yes man'—it'd be disadvantageous not to be in Soviet Russia—whispered something in Joseph's ear, and the duo walked over to Thomas with evil smiles on their faces. With Stalin's hand on Thomas's shoulder, his translator said "Secretary says, 'It takes one to know one.'"

And like that, the Russian leader and his translator made their way back to their respective seats. One of the most brutal dictators to walk the face of the planet had retorted one wisecrack with another. There was a real chance of danger as Stalin had no issue murdering even those in his inner circle, but for one moment, he felt like showing a sense of humor. That being said, had Thomas been a Soviet citizen, it surely would have been gulag or death, and that was a clear double-standard, and he knew it. But being a young, flip-mouthed foreign kid and telling one of the world's most powerful men what he was something he'd never forget. Humor has a way of breaking down the walls that divide people, and if Stalin could laugh at a smart-assed American kid calling him a cuss word, then maybe the world wasn't as horrible as it appeared.

Returning to his seat with the main course served, Thomas couldn't wait to tell his family—especially Brian—what he had just done.

"I met Stalin back there. I saw him when I was walking out of the restroom," Thomas proclaimed.

"I hope you were polite to the secretary," Matthew said, taking a bite of the fowl—which he assumed was pheasant—the main course of the meal.

"Actually, I said something that made him laugh," Thomas said, knowing there was no place for foul language at the dinner table.

"That's nice," Craig said, while also trying to figure out what this form of poultry was.

Brian nudged Thomas on the shoulder and whispered, "What'd you *really* say?" knowing damn well that it wasn't a 'knock, knock' joke.

"I called him an asshole, and his translator translated it for him," Thomas said, just loud enough for Brian to hear but not at a level his parents or aunt and uncle could hear.

"And you're still breathing?" Brian answered, knowing Stalin had no issue killing family members, much less foreigners with big mouths and nothing to back them up.

"Yes, sir; he told me, via his translator, that it took one to know one," Thomas answered, as if he was recounting a play from a ball game that morning.

The two families left the party early and went right to Matthew and Katlyn's dacha, where, despite having packed up all their bags, there was plenty of booze to be consumed. While the parents were putting down bottle after bottle of brandy and Georgian wine, their sons sat outside by the pool and took in what turned out to be a lovely summer evening in the capital of communism.

"I still can't believe you said that to Stalin," Brian said.

"I honestly can't wait to tell Anna tomorrow," Thomas replied. He and Anna had had a few other rendezvous at the park—unbeknownst to Brian—and they'd developed a bit of a rapport. If his charm and her beauty could break the ice between the free world and a communist state, then maybe there was some good in the world.

"I thought you were leaving tomorrow morning?"

"I am, but she said she'd say bye before we left," Thomas said, looking and sounding like Cary Grant.

"You're good. You come into town for ten days, and you've got the prettiest girl in Russia meeting you to see you off after you call the secretary a foul word," Brian said with the most obvious hint of jealousy in his voice. Brian may have been a smart kid, but his slightly older cousin had him beaten in the self-confidence department.

The sunlight cracking through the window of the dacha woke Thomas and opened yet another day that was a weird mix of beauty-Anna-and the definition of beastly-Stalin. Thomas was excited his family was beginning their quest back to America and away from this place. He was also glad to have one more chance to see Anna, whom he'd grown quite fond of.

He went out to the park not far from the dacha, where he told Anna he'd be, and waited. The waiting continued as the early morning turned into almost noon as plenty of people passed by, but not one of them was Anna. She was nowhere to be found, but at the very place Thomas said to meet, there stood a smug Captain Folanov.

"What happened to Anna?" an angry Thomas shouted at the NKVD officer, whose heart of stone was painfully apparent by now.

"She went somewhere—a vacation, as I believe you Americans call it," Captain Folanov said, with absolutely no emotion.

"You're absolutely fucking despicable," Thomas said as he began to tear up at the thought of what happened to the beautiful Russian girl he'd hit it off with.

"I am taking you back to the dacha. One more word, though, and you go the way she went," Folanov said as he grabbed Thomas the way a constable would take a youngster who had been caught underage drinking or stealing fruit from a store.

The Russian officer and his American "prisoner" walked down the street and right into the backyard of the dacha, where Matthew and Katlyn stood.

"Where the hell have you been, and what is going on?" Matthew asked as he saw his son being held by the collar by the ruthless Russian.

"I was supposed to meet Anna, but they took her away," Thomas said. Folanov released his grip, and Thomas ran into the arms of his mother.

"She went somewhere else. She didn't like your son, I'm sure," Folanov said, his story changing like the weather.

By now, Matthew—someone who had fought Russian communists once upon a time and held them in low regard—was seething, and fired back at the Russian. "You lying sack of shit. You know damn well where she went, and you're not telling us."

"I don't have to tell you anything; you are a guest in our country and have no right to dictate how we operate in the Soviet Union. Maybe if your son didn't attempt to show up our leader last night, this wouldn't be an issue," Captain Folanov said without so much as batting an eyelash.

"Your country sucks, and so does communism," Thomas said in a tone of voice that screamed, *I don't give a fuck what happens to me*. Subconsciously, he also felt Anna's blood was on his hands, and if it meant his own demise, then so be it. Matthew's firm grip on Thomas's arms were the only thing that kept the young man from physically lunging at the smug KGB operator.

"Your son needs to watch his comments. Russian boys would never speak out of turn like that, nor would they ever talk to a leader like he did," Folanov said, as he showed his talents weren't limited to torturing innocent people—he could lecture people on how to raise their kids as well.

"FUCK RUSSIA, FUCK STALIN!" the livid Thomas hurled at the ever emotionless Folanov. In his eyes, all bets were off, and the time for doing anything that resembled playing nice in the sandbox went right out the window.

"THOMAS, ENOUGH!" Katlyn said, not wanting to see her son hauled off to a Siberian gulag, too.

"I think it best for you that you leave our country and spew your falsities about the great communist system and our fearless leader in your own country," Folanov said.

"It's your lucky day, asshole, we're leaving today. I should have greased more of you back in Vladivostok. I'll have you know, I disobeyed engagement orders and, on a few occasions, smoked a few of your countrymen," Matthew said, openly bragging about his exploits during the American expedition in Siberia—something he'd never really done to Katlyn or Thomas.

"America saw the need to get involved and lost," Folanov fired back, referencing the failed intervention of the World War I allied powers to stop communism in its cradle almost two decades earlier. "Communism won then, and it will win again in time. Nice try, tough guy."

"What did I miss?" Craig said as he, Maryalice, and Brian all arrived on the scene, intending to see their family members off but somehow walking into a potential international incident, with verbal bomb after verbal bomb being dropped.

"Anna was taken away, and this asshole clearly knows where and why and won't fill us in," Matthew said to his brother.

"As you know, Mr. Whitney, we don't have to tell you or anyone else—especially foreigners—anything about how and why we do things," Folanov said in the same condescending and emotionless tone.

"I'm applying for a transfer somewhere else within the State Department. This country is fucked. Franklin has to know how bad things are over here and to avoid any deals or alliances with you and your damn government," Craig said calmly, losing whatever faith he had in the U.S. diplomatic mission to the Soviet Union.

"What did Anna do to deserve being taken away?" Brian chimed in. "She was a nice girl and proud of being Russian."

"That does not concern you, young man. She broke the guidelines of how to be a proper Soviet and must suffer the consequences. Your little friend here might know a little more," Folanov said to the American teenager.

"One of the cars from the embassy is picking you guys up to take you to the station. Should be here within the hour. What's your itinerary after that?" Craig said, as he served as a bit of a travel agent for his brother's family in their departure from the USSR.

"Moscow to Paris, Antwerp, Antwerp to London, London to Boston, Boston to Deerfield, drop Thomas off, Deerfield to Boston, Boston to Chicago, Chicago to San Diego," Matthew said, laying out just how literal the family's "trip around the world" would be.

"Damn, you're covering a lot of ground," Craig said.

"That's the beautiful thing about capitalism—you work hard and get to spend your money as *you* see fit," Matthew replied, in an attempt to show up Folanov by mocking his government while still holding back his teenage son from attacking the Russian, which would earn the boy a one-way ticket to the executioner.

Folanov didn't take the bait. "I hope you enjoyed your time here in the Soviet Union, but it is time you go," he said before withdrawing back into his guest house.

"This is my fault," Thomas said as the tears began rolling down his face. "If I hadn't said what I said to Stalin last night, there's no way they'd have taken her."

"I thought you told him a joke," Mary Alice said, as she recounted the now hazy events from the night before. Several bottles of vodka on the rocks will do that to you.

"I called him an asshole, and his translator translated it for him," Thomas began. He may have thought of himself as a bad boy, but up to now, the mere thought of cussing in front of Matthew and Katlyn gave him shivers. "He laughed and told me it took one to know one. I thought he was kidding with me and nothing would happen."

Matthew was confused and disgusted by his son's behavior. There are certain actions no parent wants to hear that their child has done, and cussing at a world leader—one known to be butcher of the innocent—qualifies as one of them.

"You called Stalin an asshole, and thought there'd be zero blowback?" Matthew yelled. "You're kidding me, right?"

"This isn't America, Thomas," his uncle chimed in, knowing his nephew had likely made his job at the embassy that much harder. "There's no First Amendment. You're lucky it's not you who's gone missing. You're my nephew and godson, and I love you unconditionally, but this could have caused an international incident. Think before you speak, kid."

"I should've known better," Thomas sobbed.

"You're damn right you should have. You shoot your mouth off to look like a wise guy, and an innocent girl ends up likely dead."

Before Thomas could add to his solemn apology, Craig once again chimed in. "That's not necessarily the case," he said. "Stalin's been picking people off with ties to the embassy for a while. I'm not saying your pride and joy helped her cause, but the government seems to have a strong dislike for citizens interacting with foreigners. That's why we've told Brian to stay away from the Russian students at the American School—once they interact with foreigners, there's a bullseye on their backs, and that's not fair to them."

"They distrust foreigners, murder their own people, and have suppression of anything resembling free thought or speech," Matthew yelled. "I can't say enough how fucked this place really is. This is right out of a Huxley novel for Christ's sake."

"We're working on getting out of here before the end of the year," Craig said. "If Franklin wants relations with this country, then good on him, but I cannot and will not be a part of this charade. Seeing it happen firsthand to an innocent school girl is sickening." Craig knew he had the clout to land another assignment at his choice of locations.

As they said their goodbyes, a car from the embassy pulled up to whisk the California Whitneys to the train station in Moscow, where their journey back to the U.S. would begin.

"I wouldn't say it was a great time, but thank you for hosting my family and I," Matthew said as he embraced both his brother and sister-in-law before loading up the car.

"I wish things had gone a little bit differently, but thank you for coming," Craig replied.

"Uncle Craig, I'm sorry for causing you so much trouble on the way out the door," a still-tearful Thomas said as he approached his godfather with his hand outstretched.

"Listen, don't take this whole thing to heart," Craig answered, moving Thomas's hand away and instead embracing him in a big hug. "You didn't kidnap Anna, a flawed, maniacal regime did. This country is completely fucked. That goes far beyond you."

Moving on from his godfather, Thomas sought out Brian and gave his cousin a hug. "All things considered, it *was* good to see you."

"I agree. I'll see you Stateside soon, I'm sure," Brian answered as Thomas got into the embassy's livery.

As the car pulled away from the dacha, Thomas was still almost paralyzed with grief. His big mouth and borderline reckless attitude may have cost Anna her very life. He needed to make changes to himself in the process of growing up—like everyone does—but his situation was different than your average American teenager. His actions may have cost a young woman her life, but was it his fault? He was in a foreign country that was the antithesis of the United States. But did that matter? He had plenty of time to sit in silence and think about the cause and effect of his actions and how he should change himself for the better.

***

Eastern German Frontier

August 6, 1935

Traveling across Europe and seeing what it has to offer should be a bucket list item for every American. At the ripe old age of seventeen, during one of the United States' worst depressions, Thomas Whitney was getting a great view—from a passenger car. The endless journey allowed his brain to turn the events that lead to Anna's disappearance over and over in his head. The line between absolution and accountability continued to be blurred in his young mind as he reminded himself over and over again that Stalin and his communist thugs were truly the ones to blame for what happened to Anna, and all he did was set off the powder keg.

"At least this is more scenic than the ride across Russia," Thomas said, breaking an awkward silence that had hung over the family since they left Moscow.

"We'll be going through Berlin soon. It's one of the most talked about cities in the world these days," Matthew replied.

"That Hitler guy is the president, right?" Thomas asked, trying to start a conversation.

"He's the Fuhrer, so pretty much. He's got the country back to work and is mobilizing its military again. I'd be afraid if I was Stalin right now."

"So, you're saying this Hitler guy and the German army are the world's best hope against communism?" Thomas asked, imagining the brown-coated German soldiers laying waste to Stalin and his communist regime in the process.

"He's a threat to Western Europe and maybe the US, too. We'll see how the British and French handle him. I'm sure they hate communism as much as we do, but seeing a strong German army isn't in their best interests either—you know what happened last time," Matthew answered, as he in so many words communicated to his son that the world was far from black and white. Though a militarized Germany may be bad for communist Russia, it was far from ideal for the rest of the world, too as Britain, France, potentially even the United States could fall under Hitler's crosshairs.

While Matthew was lecturing him on the clusterfuck that is European politics, Thomas looked out the window of the train—which had come to a stop at a station. Outside, he saw a number of young men, barely older than he was, in perfect formation and in uniforms that were as meticulous as they were intimidating.

"That's the new and improved Werchmacht right there," Matthew said, looking out the window at the young soldiers. "There'll be another war within the next five or ten years."

"Why do you sound so sure about that?" Thomas asked.

"The Treaty of Versailles left Germany in a tough spot financially, militarily, and hurt their national pride. Hitler has them up and running domestically, and their military is getting there. They're not gonna sit tight for long."

Thomas quickly did the math in his head. He was seventeen, and the five- to ten-year window would put him between twenty-two and twenty-seven when the "action" started—prime military age. "I have a feeling I'll be back here again," he whispered to himself as he took one last look at the waves of German soldiers.

***

Deerfield Academy, Massachusetts

August 20, 1935

Thousands of miles away from Stalin's terror—and a continent that was due to explode like a powder keg for the second time in two decades—the Whitney family had one last moment together. The proud parents moved Thomas into his dormitory at Deerfield Academy and prepared to make the trip back to California. They had left San Diego eight weeks earlier, spent nearly four weeks traveling, and had seen all of the world they wanted to—or for that matter, needed to—see. Football practice began first thing in the morning the next day, so it was time for the elder Whitneys to say goodbye.

"I hope you never forget what you saw over there in Russia, and remember that no matter what we think of our president, life here is better than anywhere else," Matthew said as he gave his son one last look up and down. While he was still disappointed in his son's behavior and its consequences, he felt strangely proud. Deep down in places he'd like to forget existed, Matthew knew his son's unfiltered gall would get his son further in life than the conformity that everyone expected of him. Well-behaved men who went with the flow and never spoke out of turn would never change the world, and he knew his contrary son's destiny was to make big waves.

"Yes, I'm just thinking about getting on the field tomorrow."

He was lying right through his teeth—Russia, and the evils of Stalin had been on the forefront of his mind since they left Moscow. On the other hand, he *was* looking forward to getting on the football field and showing his new classmates and teammates what he could do.

"As you should be," his father replied. "Remember: keep your head up when you're on the field and down in the books when it's time for studies. You've got the whole world at your fingertips. Don't forget what I've always told you."

"Yes, of course. 'To whom much is given, much is expected,'" Thomas said, with the same enthusiasm with which he brushed his teeth in the morning.

Katlyn left the room first, so father and son had a moment to themselves for the first time on the trip, and Thomas wanted to make the most of it.

"What happened in Russia when you were in the service?" he asked, hoping to get the unabridged version before his father had to leave.

Matthew took a deep breath and remembered stepping off the gangway into Vladivostok Harbor almost twenty years earlier. "I shipped out a few months after you were born, in 1918. I signed up because Woodrow Wilson made it sound like we'd be slaying this great German Hun that threatened our freedom, and I was all in. Instead of going to France like your Uncle Craig, I got sent to Vladivostok as part of some stupid 'expeditionary force' that had no real objectives. Most of the time we were over there, we were waiting, but after a few months, I got bored, and at night, I would sneak out past the allied lines with some of the Cossacks in the area and try to pop a few communist forces."

"So you disobeyed orders, just to fight communism?" Thomas asked. This was the most he had ever heard about his father's service in Russia.

"Yeah, I had read Karl Marx's garbage book while I was still at Stanford. I had developed an intense hatred for Marxism. I didn't want it to take hold anywhere. In my eyes, it was sheer and utter madness—the mere concept of 'Communist Russia' was something we needed to put a kibosh to early on. For Marxism to take hold anywhere would be unfortunate, but in the world's largest country, it would be a tragedy. Of course, being an idealist in the U.S. Army isn't exactly encouraged, and that's why I don't have the Purple Heart I rightfully deserve."

"What do you mean?"

"Toward the end of my time in Russia, I got shot doing one of my illegal and unsanctioned missions and had to tell my commanding officer it happened while training on the firing range. There was no way I'd get an award for reckless training, but it did help me get home earlier."

"How bad did you get shot?" Thomas said, as his view of his father changed from him being a boring, white collar, country club type to an action hero.

"One rifle shot in the shoulder—a clean hit. It was a light skirmish a few miles from our barracks on the Trans-Siberian Railroad, against bandits that were sympathetic to the Red Army. It's ironic I was on the same railroad almost twenty years later with your mother and you last month on what was supposed to be a leisurely vacation," Matthew said, as he moved his polo shirt to reveal the wound that Thomas had seen before but never thought to ask about.

"Did you notice any of the landmarks near where you got shot when we were riding through Siberia?"

"God, no, whole place looks the same. Besides, I tried to forget about that whole experience once I got back Stateside. Honestly, I never really thought about it until we were over here on our little family vacation."

"Matthew, they don't have classes for men over forty here, so it's time to get going," Katlyn said as she came back into the room and unintentionally butted into a deep father-son heart-to-heart.

"Of course," Matthew said as he embraced his son one last time before heading out the door.

Thomas watched them pull away in their car and realized for the first time he was on his own, 3,000 miles from where he grew up. At seventeen, he was tasked with continuing his family's legacy at Deerfield, while also making a name for himself, far from the comforts of southern California. Because despite all that had had happened in Russia, he was still just an American high school senior-a far cry from being the guy that called a ruthless dictator an asshole a few weeks earlier.

***

French Frontier

October 17, 1943

0600 hours

For all of the woods and hills that Thomas and Rebecca had seen during their trek to freedom, they had yet to find a five-star resort, meaning it would be yet another day of sleeping at the base of trees with rocks as pillows and hoping to God their proverbial "do not disturb" was honored. While the pair of travelers weren't friends yet, they were getting along, and the life or death circumstances of their situation made it only natural that they'd confide in each other.

"I never went camping as a kid," Thomas said, thinking aloud as the two settled in. "My Mom thought sleeping outside was primitive and would never let me go. She said sleeping in a tent when you can have a roof over your head was idiotic. I'll tell you—I wish I had a tent right now."

"Some warm cover and an even warmer meal in a safe place would be amazing right now," Rebecca said. She wasn't asking for much—just warmth and for the people who wanted her dead to just go away.

As Thomas began dozing off, unable to sustain conversation about his wilderness experience—or lack thereof—Rebecca began thinking about the rudimentary living situation that had defined her and her family's existence for over two years.

Besancon, France

May 11, 1941

The Couture family had lived a charmed existence in Besancon. Patriarch Vincent taught at the local university, his wife Chelsea—a native of London, whom he met at Oxford—was a talented musician. Their oldest daughter, Ariella, was living in Bern, just over the border in Switzerland, and was engaged to be married to a prominent Swiss banker. Their youngest daughter, Rebecca, was set to attend Oxford and begin the second generation of Coutures to attend the prestigious English institution. That all changed when German tanks rolled through the streets of Besançon in the summer of 1940. Rather than attend Oxford, Rebecca was forced to stay home and commiserate about the lousy timing of her life. Both Vincent and Chelsea were forced to leave their jobs as a result of Vincent's Jewish background. By May of 1941, the discrimination had turned to outright persecution, as Jews throughout France were being rounded up by the Gestapo. The whispers had grown louder and louder, and it was time for Vincent to put his family into hiding.

Rebecca and Chelsea sat at the kitchen table, wondering when—not if—the door would burst open and the Gestapo would take them off to an unknown fate. Vincent walked into the room and laid out how they would avoid being dragged away by the evil forces of the occupying German army. "We leave tonight. We're going into hiding rather than letting these Nazis just drag us away."

"Where are we going?" Chelsea asked. It seemed tickets out of hell weren't exactly falling down like manna from Heaven.

"The LaFleurs are going to hide us in their basement for the duration of all this," Vincent said, knowing any semblance of the luxury they'd become used to would become a distant memory. "I've spoken to Nicholas, and he has set it up for us. There's room for three, and no semblance of plumbing."

"How long will that be for?" Rebecca asked. She knew her already turned-upside-down world was about to take a further turn for the worse.

"I don't know," Vincent said, realizing their stay in his friends' basement would likely be for the duration of the German occupation—if they were lucky enough to avoid being captured— but not wanting his children to worry, "but get a small bag together and let's go. We have no time to waste."

"Why can't we go to Bern and live with Ariella?" Rebecca asked, as the reality of spending the next few months—or possibly, years—living in a basement was anything but appealing.

"They'll stop us at the border," Chelsea chimed in as she began putting a few essentials in her bag and got ready to go.

"Nicholas is outside in his car," Vincent said. "He and Marie said we need to be quiet while we're staying there. Their young son Charles's youthful curiosity could get us in trouble if he heard us."

As they poured into Nicholas's car, Rebecca took one last look at the house her family had called home. A foreign army had come to town, and their anti-Jewish policies had forced her from all she'd ever known.

As they pulled up in front of the LaFleurs's home, they were shuffled through the bulkhead into the place the family would be living for the foreseeable future.

"Make yourselves at home," Nicholas whispered as he made his way back. "Marie and I will be dropping off food and making sure you're as comfortable as you can be a couple times per week. We'll be as secretive about this as possible—and you should be as quiet as possible— to avoid arousing any suspicion from Charles. I'm worried he's too young and curious to keep a secret like this."

"So, this is home," Rebecca said as she examined the somewhat spacious basement that had three cots, blankets, a few loaves of bread, and a bucket that would serve as a toilet in a room where privacy was nonexistent. In another life, she'd be at Oxford, studying and enjoying

he simpler things in England. Now, she'd be getting her PhD in survival and trying to turn a
hellish situation into one where we she could come out alive.

French Frontier

October 17, 1943

1130 hours

Thomas had awoken from his early morning snooze and was now on guard duty as Rebecca tried to get in at least a little sleep. As she woke up for a brief second from her slumber, she had another confession to make to Thomas.

"It sounds so wrong to say after all that has happened, but being out and on the run makes me feel more alive than I ever have," Rebecca whispered as she adjusted herself and sat up against the tree she was lying under.

"How's that?" Thomas asked, not really caring but also not wanting to be rude.

"Fresh air for a change is very good, and being able to actually avoid capture instead of sitting around and hoping the Nazis never find you is liberating. Running is better than hiding. Isn't that what they say in America?"

"Something like that," Thomas said, realizing she was thinking of the old idiom, *you can run, but you can't hide.*

"You never answered the question I asked you when we first met," Thomas said. "Why didn't you make a run for the border sooner?"

Rebecca, off the top of her head, had no really good answer. For years, her and her parents sat in a dingy basement and ate the LaFleurs' table scraps. A break for the border was never even laid out on the table. "I don't know. Maybe we just thought our chances of hiding were better than our chances of running."

As she uttered that loosely translated phrase once again, she was taken back to the feelings she had when she turned from a hider into a runner.

Besançon, France

October 11, 1943

2130 hours

Living as a refugee in a cellar for years without so much as a gasp of fresh air can drive a person mad. The Coutures had plenty of reading material, and the LaFleurs always gave them books and newspapers to keep them occupied. Reading smuggled-in books and newspapers was the only thing that gave the family any taste of the world outside their basement. Their hosts tried to make the Coutures feel as comfortable as possible, but that task was monumental, if not impossible. Not only had the world around them descended into chaos, but shielding Charles from much of the madness—including the presence of their house guests—was a daunting task. During the day, while Charles was away at school, the Coutures could use the washroom, but during the majority of the time, they were confined to their underground dungeon.

It was a seasonally frigid night where a sudden drop in temperature made it feel even cooler than it actually was. Not even layer upon layer of blankets could keep the cold from the cellar. Rebecca tossed and turned and wished she had her parents' ability to simply fall asleep under even the worst of circumstances. She'd had enough, and decided to sneak out via the bulkhead door and get some fresh air for the first time since she could remember. The cold made it a less than ideal night to grab some fresh air, but Rebecca couldn't wait any longer. Looking into the starry sky and woods that surrounded the LaFleur home gave her a brief escape from the hell that had engulfed her life and the world. She thought about simply breaking for the Swiss border, but simply walking east through Nazi occupied territory wasn't exactly advisable. Her living conditions may not have been ideal, but they were just that—living conditions. She had her life, and that was more than plenty of her fellow countrymen could say. Likewise, she couldn't just leave her parents behind and run away into the night. Sitting tight wasn't perfect, but it had kept her alive up to this point.

As she turned to return to the cellar where her parents still slept, Rebecca felt she was being watched. Looking up, she caught Charles's tiny eyes looking at her through his bedroom window. The youngster was supposed to be asleep, but something had woken him. She went back inside, knowing the youngster had seen her, but she hoped he would think it was a dream. Her cot was calling her name, but she laid there awake for much of the night, wondering how the young boy would handle seeing someone enter his home. The cellar setup helped hide them— there was no access point to the basement within the house, only the bulkhead and rudimentary tunnel that had been constructed. The narrow tunnel that led to the wooded area about thirty yards from the house itself had been constructed almost by accident. When the family first moved in, Vincent had begun chiseling into the side of the wall out of boredom, and he eventually formed a tiny crawlspace. Over time, with the help of the other Coutures, he constructed an escape hole in the woods at the end of the tunnel, covered by a piece of plywood, with leaves to camouflage it. The dirt from the tunnel was then spread around elsewhere on the property as not to raise any more suspicions. On the inside, an old painting covered up the hole, which was just big enough to fit an adult but also gave the basement a frigid draft in the winter. Vincent and Chelsea judged it to be worth the drawbacks—in the event that the Gestapo found their tiny refuge, it would give them a shot in hell of escaping.

Despite feeling the rush of fresh air in her lungs and savoring every second, Rebecca wondered what her little excursion would mean for her and her family's future.

Besançon

October 15, 1943

1350 hours

Vibrations could be felt like tremors in the basement as what sounded like multiple vehicles—likely large trucks—moved toward the LaFleur house. Vincent had a feeling this wasn't a joyous trip, and his face quickly gave that away to his wife and daughter.

"What should we do?" Chelsea asked.

"Get Rebecca in the tunnel! Every second counts!" Vincent knew it was unlikely all three of them could be saved, but there *could* be just enough time for his daughter to at least have a chance at life.

"What about you?" Rebecca asked as she moved toward the painting that that hid the passage out of the cellar and to freedom.

"We'll be fine! Just get in there now! Every second counts," Vincent replied.

There was no time for debate as Vincent quickly moved the painting out of the way and pushed his daughter into the crawl space.

"I love you," she said with tears in her eyes as she began crawling through the dirty tunnel. It was far from stable, and one wrong move could lead to its collapse on her, but that was the furthest thing from her mind.

"We love you, too. Get out of here," Vincent said as he caught one last glimpse of his daughter and moved the grandfather clock back to cover up the hole. He looked and saw his wife on her knees, praying to anyone that would listen, and he, too, knelt and asked for divine intervention.

Gunfire and screams were heard upstairs as the Nazis punished the LaFleurs for their humanity—there was no judge or jury, but there clearly were executioners. Within thirty seconds of shots ringing out, the door to the basement had been kicked in, and the Nazi thugs had swarmed the family's living quarters.

Meanwhile, thirty yards away, Rebecca was poking her head out from the tunnel and pulling herself through it. She was still close enough to the house that she could hear the screams, and she was well within rifle range, so she started running.

Once she was far enough from the tunnel opening and in the middle of the woods, Rebecca let the tears flow. She knew there could be German patrols anywhere, but she didn't have the emotional stability right now to care. Her family was surely hauled away from their hiding spot and en route to a death camp somewhere, if the Gestapo hadn't murdered them first. Hers wasn't the only family that was now ruined, as the LaFleurs were now paying the price for harboring a Jewish family. They showed basic humanity and compassion and died for it. "Where was the caring and goodness in the world?" she wondered.

"How did they find us?" Rebecca asked herself as she began moving again, wiping the tears off her face.

She figured Charles had probably said something to a schoolmate, by accident more than likely, that got back to the authorities. Nicholas and Marie had surely told their boy to keep quiet about what was going on in their home, that their houseguests were not to be discussed, but in this case, an innocent mistake cost them all their lives. Rebecca couldn't hold herself to be angry at the youngster, and she understood why his parents tried to shield their boy from what was happening in the basement.

Rebecca kept moving through the dense shrubby forest. She knew the road to freedom would involve her going east to the Swiss border, where hopefully, Ariella was waiting for her.

French Frontier

October 17, 1943

1950 hours

"When you get to freedom, what's the first thing you want to do?" Rebecca asked as they moved out for what they hoped would be one last night on the lam.

"Shower, shave, and get some food and a cup of coffee," Thomas said. He'd never again take for granted the once simple joy of pressing a cup of joe to his lips. An Italian submarine sandwich with all the fixings didn't sound too bad, either, as he promised himself he'd never go more than a day without eating ever again.

"Of all the things that were horrible about living in that dark and dreary basement, one thing I missed the most was music. We had to leave our fancy record player at home when we went into hiding, and I miss the sound of it. I love the classics—Mozart especially."

"I'm more of a Bing Crosby, Frank Sinatra guy, or I used to be, anyway."

"I've never heard Sinatra. Is he any good?"

"He's *okay,* I guess," Thomas said as he thought back to the last time he actually listened to any Sinatra.

US Eighth Air Force Headquarters, Britain

October 11, 1943

2245 hours

According to the higher-ups, the squadron's latest mission over France had been a success, as the bombers had completed their objective with no one shot down. The same couldn't be said for the fighter pilots who lost one of their own over hostile skies. Lieutenant Danny Edelman was liked throughout the squadron, and his death was a shock to his friends. He was among the first to "welcome" Tyler and Thomas to the unit, and he made them feel at home despite being an ocean away from the comforts of America. This shared respect convinced the pilots to give him an impromptu memorial service at the officer's club when they got back to England.

"Here's to Lieutenant Edelman, a small guy that had a big heart and even bigger balls," Major Leney said as he raised a toast for his fallen pilot before calling it a night early, allowing his subordinates to carry on unchaperoned. He knew they could be an all-time band of lunatics, but he also trusted them to make responsible decisions.

While the pilots drank to remember their friend and forget the visual of watching his plane explode, Thomas grew angrier and angrier at the music coming from the record player. A few Sinatra songs in a row infuriated the pilot, who viewed Ol' Blue Eyes as a coward. He was at home while other men his age—like Lieutenant Edelman—gave their lives for the war effort. Within minutes, his face had turned beet red; he was visibly seething as he sat alone at the end of the bar. While Sinatra had yet to achieve the levels of success that would define his life career Thomas had come across some of his records by chance and quickly became a fan. With each day in a combat zone and each young life he saw lost, his contempt for the New Jersey Casanova grew more and more.

"Turn this fucking shit off," a drunken Thomas said as he forcefully removed the record from the player and smashed it over his knee—embarrassingly falling down in his drunken stupor in the process.

"What's your problem, lieutenant? Because I'm about ten seconds away from calling the MPs, so it better be a really big problem," the officer's lounge captain said to him. Thomas brought himself to his feet and sloppily put up what could generously be called a salute.

"My problem? You want to know my problem?" Thomas began with rage before taking a deep breath and calming himself down. "I'm over here getting shot at over Europe on a daily basis, watching my buddies get incinerated a mile up, and we're listening to this asshole. Who, by the way, took the easy road out of serving in this war because of some bullshit ear condition that had him labelled 4-F. Hell, I wish my ears were 4-F so I wouldn't have to listen to this bullshit you people call music."

"It's not Sinatra's fault he was 4-F," the captain said, trying to calm down the seething pilot and defend Frank's honor.

"I was 4-F, too, but I had the resolve to fight. Where's the no-good guinea bastard right now? Banging his way through Hollywood and telling everyday Americans to buy fucking war bonds. Really great service to the country. Hell, most women are doing more to win the war than the damn wop. I don't see him working long, thankless hours in a factory to keep the American war machine rolling."

Thomas looked at the captain in charge and realized the error in his drunken ways. "I'm sorry, sir. If you want to send me to the brig, I understand."

"I see you boys lost one of your friends today. I'll let this slide and chalk it up to a few too many. Go to your barracks, get some sleep, and don't make me regret this," the captain calmly offered.

"You won't regret it," Thomas said as he composed himself and sought to put his drunken fight with a record behind him.

Thomas was grateful and scurried out the door into his bunk, where he slept off his drunkenness.

As he woke up with a heavy head, he caught Lieutenant Donovan—ever the Spartan—doing a set of push-ups on the floor.

"Does the army pay you more if you get up early and exercise?" Thomas asked, still in bed with a throbbing headache.

"Nope, but it looks unkindly upon morons that cause disruptions in officer's clubs over the choice of music," Tyler said as he finished his set and sat down on his bunk.

"You heard about that?"

"Tom, I was right there when it happened. Just hope to God Leney doesn't hear about it, or else you're fucked. No weekend passes to go gallivanting in London for you. Hell, he might follow through and make you scrub dishes while we grease Krauts."

"I'm too valuable to the war effort; no way in hell he takes my wings away. Speaking of that, I've got a twenty-four-hour pass effective at twelve-hundred. Nothing but British stouts and the fine ladies of the women's auxiliary corps for a full day."

"My God, raise your standards. You're from money—act like it for God's sake," Lieutenant Donovan said as he wrapped up his mini-workout and took a seat on the bunk.

"Sure, none of them are Rita Hayworth, but it's the best you can get in a damn warzone," Thomas said.

"I'm talking about your choice of beverage. English stouts are too sweet. Irish stouts are the way to go. Get yourself a Guinness and really live it."

"Ordering an Irish beer *in* England. Only you Donovan," Thomas said as he tried to fall back asleep for at least a few more moments.

"I hope we get called for a mission and your pass gets revoked. Maybe a brewery will be accidentally bombed, because that's the closest thing you'll get to a cold one tonight."

"It'd be the definition of bad things happening to good people."

"No, it would be the exact opposite of that. You're the kind of guy that rolls in shit and comes out smelling like a rose. It'd be nice to see your gallivanting catch up with you."

Hungover, Thomas looked forward to when his pass went into effect so he could use the hair of the dog to have an enjoyable day not thinking about the war. Like so much else in war, that was about to come crashing down in more ways than one.

"Can you wait here and give me some privacy while I use a tree as a washroom?" Rebecca embarrassingly asked.

"Are you sure you don't want me to come and keep guard?"

"Absolutely not! I'll take my chances with whatever is in these woods than give you the benefit of seeing me like that. Besides, I can take care of myself."

"Suit yourself," Thomas shrugged. It wasn't the first, nor would it be the last, time a woman wanted privacy around him.

Thomas wanted to give her space, but he also didn't want to run the risk of getting separated in the dense woods, so he kept a safe, but close-enough distance.

The hairs on the back of Thomas's neck stood at attention, and a chill seeped through his skin. He had the feeling that the pair was not alone. Less than a second later, he heard a twig split—something, or someone, was there with them—and he went into a crouch behind a tree, ducking enough to *just* be out of sight.

"Please be a fucking deer," Thomas whispered to himself. It became clearer and clearer by the second that this wasn't a furry forest animal, but rather, a pair of fellow human beings. Their helmets became visible, and Thomas realized he was closer to an enemy soldier than he ever wanted to be. He'd flown many missions over Europe and been above the madness, but now he came face-to-face with the enemy.

The two wehrmacht soldiers were now between him and Rebecca, and they'd more than likely walk right into her. He reached for his military-issued pistol and had a sobering realization that Rebecca had the *good* pistol, and he was left with Lieutenant Brady's old west revolver which, like so many other relics, had seen better days.

As they got closer to Rebecca, Thomas quietly followed them. As he got closer, a shot rang out from a bush that grazed one German solider and caused them both to begin firing in all directions. Luckily for Thomas and Rebecca, they had bolt action rifles and not automatic weapons, meaning they couldn't just spray fire.

"I wish I actually tried this thing out on the range," Thomas said as he sprung up and opened fire on the pair of enemy soldiers, missing his target but hitting the other one by accident At that exact moment, Rebecca emerged from the same bush with his GI pistol and fired another shot right into the chest of the remaining German. He fell beside his comrade as the recoil planted her on her backside. Both were still alive.

"Fuck this," Thomas said as he sprinted toward the downed German soldiers and fired another round, this time taking one out.

Rebecca then jumped on the last German soldier and shot him at point-blank range, causing blood to splatter everywhere.

"Are you alright?" a bloody Rebecca asked Thomas as she got up and admired her work.

"I'm fine, but why the fuck did you open fire?"

"They were getting closer, I had a gun, and I wasn't going to let them do to me what they did to my family."

"Now we're really fucking in it," Thomas said as the panic in his voice became apparent. He didn't know how close the other German troops were. They probably weren't far, and they'd have to be deaf to miss the gunfire.

"War is easy for you from your planes, but here on the ground, it comes down to this. I'm glad these two fucks are dead. I hope to kill more of them for what they've done to me and so many others in their quest to terrorize the world."

"Grab what you can from the bodies, and let's get out of here. This place could be swarming with more of them any second," Thomas said, not wanting them both to be caught.

"If I ever get back to England, the guys will go nuts when they see this," Thomas said as he took one of the German's side arms—a luger—and put it in his inside pocket. He then picked up one of their rifles and grabbed ammunition from both bodies. If more troops were coming, he'd be ready with more firepower. "Wish the Krauts had food on them because I'm fucking famished."

"I've never shot a gun before," Rebecca said as she examined the bodies one last time before turning to Thomas.

"How'd you know what to do?" he asked.

"Point and pull the trigger. Not that hard. It felt good, except for the blowback, which I wasn't quite expecting."

Outside of their guns and ammunition, the dead bodies provided next to no real value, except as a rag as Rebecca used one of their meticulously woven uniforms to wipe some of the blood off herself.

"I take it red isn't your color," Thomas remarked as Rebecca tried to get at least some of the German blood off her.

"Much as I wish I could bathe in the blood of these pieces of shit, it smells awful and feels uncomfortable."

As they prepared to flee the scene of the shootout, Thomas couldn't help but examine the revolver that served him well despite its shortcomings. "Talk about a lucky hand. Wish that crazy bastard Brady could see me right now."

Moving through the woods at a somewhat frantic pace, both to get away from their kill counts and toward the ever closer border, the pace of Thomas and Rebecca was different. This was no longer about moving slowly, but surely, it was now about getting to the border as quickly as possible. During their almost-sprint, two more figures appeared across the woods, and Thomas was ready for yet another engagement.

"It's deja-fucking-vu," he remarked as he and Rebecca knelt down and hoped for the best. They had been lucky the first time around when it came to fighting the German soldiers, but he didn't like their odds of going against the Wehrmacht again.

The figures, barely visible in the twilight, were armed, but they weren't German. Their clothes were too ragtag to be uniforms. Thomas and Rebecca's collective heart rates were frantic as the two young men approached the bush.

"Friends! American!" Thomas yelled, almost nonsensically, before jumping out of his crouch and standing before the two armed young men. If they were bad guys, he had just given up their hiding spot and all but assuredly signed their death warrants, but Thomas- ever the gambler- decided to roll the dice.

"Le Resistance. So good to see you," one of the young men said, slightly startled by this shadowy figure jumping out of the vegetation.

"Thomas Whitney, U.S. Army Air Force. I got shot down not far from here a few days ago."

"Jean Claude Lemieux, and he's Stefon Huet, no English for him. Who is she?"

"I'm Rebecca Couture; I can speak for myself, *merci beaucoup*."

"She's a tough one until you get to know her," Thomas added as she stood next to him. "We're trying to get to Switzerland, and we know we're not far. We just killed a pair of Germans, and I'm sure they're hot on our tail."

"We found two dead bodies a few miles from here—they must have been your doing. Good job, lieutenant."

As much as Thomas wanted to bask in the glory of the two kills, one of the two dead Germans was Rebecca's handy work. "Thank you, but she's a helluva shot herself. Killed one of the Krauts at point-blank range like it was nothing."

"Noted," Jean Pierre said as he nodded at Rebecca, which she didn't even acknowledge.

As soon as the greetings and goodwill were in order, Thomas wanted to get back to business. "I'm a downed airman, she's a Jewish refugee, and we're both trying to get to Switzerland. What do you say?"

"My Catholic mother and father wouldn't approve of me risking my life to help a Jew," Jean Pierre said, as if anti-Semitism was a rite of passage amongst French Catholics.

"You're fucking kidding me, right?" Thomas said having assumed the anti-Semitism held by a larger number of western European Catholics had been put aside given the circumstances. He was sorely mistaken.

"No, *monsieur*. She's free to help us—we love people that kill Germans, and we have Jews in our ranks—but I don't think it's wise to allocate resources to aid in her escape. Especially after what they did to Jesus," Jean Pierre added, regurgitating the same falsehood that had allowed anti-Semitism to grow and foster in Germany, France, and the rest of Catholic Europe centuries before Hitler even came to power.

"What *we* did to one of *ours* two millennia ago? How about what these Nazi fucks did to my family and countless other innocent civilians? Fuck you and your resistance," Rebecca said, as her patience went from thin to nonexistent.

Thomas couldn't help but laugh at just how screwed up the situation was. They were all on the run from an enemy that wanted to wipe them all off the map, and a petty religious difference was going to be what derailed the whole thing. "Alright, so you won't help us out because she's Jewish? Am I reading this situation right?"

"We'll gladly take you both into our ranks, but we have better things to do than help a Jew and an American get a ticket out of here. You're better off joining with us and helping us kill Nazis if you want to really make a difference in the war effort," Jean Claude said. Manpower—and womanpower—he said, was at a premium, and both Rebecca and Thomas would be more of a help to them on the ground than in the occupied territory. Likewise, mutual hatred of the Nazis wasn't enough for him to risk life and limb to help a Jewish woman get to safety. Thomas just thought his recruitment process should be a little less alienating to potential help.

Rebecca shook her head. "Why help a countrywoman in need when you can grandstand with your guns and talk about killing Nazis? Freud is right about the male complex."

"I'm almost positive Sigmund Freud is dead, for starters," Thomas began as Freud had in fact died in 1940, and for the first time in his life, he assumed the role of adult in the conversation. "Second of all, let's go our separate ways. You guys go kill some Germans and burn some Stars of David. Do whatever you guys do, and we'll make a break to the border. Maybe meet up after the war for some cognac and steaks. I'm buying."

The deal sounded good to Jean Pierre, and he stated as much. "Of course. Good luck. We hope you get to safety. We just can't take resources away from fighting the war effort to help two individuals. We hope you understand."

"We understand alright," Rebecca began before Thomas put his hand over her mouth.

"See you boys on the flipside," Thomas said as the two resistance fighters vanished back into the shrubbery.

"That could have gone worse," Rebecca said as it was a damn miracle not a single shot was fired.

"Like it or not, we're all seeking the same objective, and their means of doing so is different than ours. We don't need them. We've gotten this far on our own; we can do this," Thomas replied, trying to give her a pep talk and put the hairy situation with the French resistance behind them.

"Deal," Rebecca said as the Swiss border was now so close, yet so far away.

The two of them continued walking through the woods *just* close enough to the rough road to use it as a guide. After a few hours, just before dawn, a checkpoint appeared through the tree line.

"We're here," Thomas said as he saw both German and Swiss troops armed to the teeth on both sides of the checkpoint a few hundred yards down the road.

"Now it's a matter of getting in. Neither one of those groups is laying out the carpet for us."

"I thought the Swiss didn't have an Army," Thomas said, remembering Switzerland's unparalleled track record of neutrality.

Rebecca wanted to once again chew out her American counterpart for being so naïve and ignorant—being neutral has nothing to do with possessing a military—but now wasn't the time or place. "Apparently, they do."

"With all the fortifications, I'm shocked there aren't any flying monkeys."

"What?"

"Did you see the *Wizard of Oz*?"

"I have no idea what you're talking about," Rebecca replied.

"Good movie. Judy Garland was excellent. All the makings of a movie people will watch hundred years from now."

"I'll put it on my list," Rebecca said as they moved into position in the trees as to avoid detection.

"Let's sit tight inside the treeline for the day and try to find a soft landing spot for us to get on the other side of the border. Surely there has to be *somewhere* without a guard tower or member of the Hitler Youth watching the line like a hawk," Thomas said.

They weren't off to the see the wizard, but off to find a way out of the hell-hole they'd found themselves in. It had taken brains, heart, courage, and a strong desire to go *home*, but they were closer to safety now than they'd ever been before. If it had only been as easy as clicking a pair of slippers.

Thomas took the first watch as Rebecca dozed off almost too easily and stared down at the wooded terrain that hid the fence between the two countries. He allowed his mind to wander, as it gave him a reason to stay awake and not let exhaustion and starvation get the better of him. For a split second, he thought about leaving Rebecca there and making a break for the border on his own, but he quickly dismissed the idea. She had been just as, if not more, responsible for them getting to this point, and leaving her to the hands of the Nazis would be the ultimate betrayal. Besides, even on his own, there was no guarantee he'd make it across the border safely. He was better off with Rebecca by his side.

Then, his mind wandered off into what little he knew of Switzerland. Mostly that there was a lot of banks that held money from around the world in a tax haven. Although as Thomas and Rebecca—both products of above average upbringings—had learned, all the money in the world couldn't save you from the hell the world had become. Money, power, and prestige may get you places in peacetime, but with the whole world at war, everything had changed.

***

London, U.K.

October 1, 1943

1650 hours

Smiddy's was a bar in London that was a frequent haunt for U.S. servicemen on leave. The drinks were cold, the bartenders and servers kind, and the atmosphere friendly, if not smoky from the chain-smoking. On their first ever weekend pass to the British capital, Tyler and Thomas found themselves there, among countless other American servicemen, enjoying a different kind of draft.

"I need to hit the head. Grab us beers and get us a table," Lieutenant Donovan said as the pair of flyers navigated the crowded bar that was so overrun with Americans it felt like a joint in New York or Chicago and not on the other side of the Atlantic.

"Anything particular?"

"Cold," Tyler replied in his usual simple, yet direct manner.

"Two of your coldest brews," Thomas said to the bartender.

"Certainly, sir. That'll be twenty cents."

"You take American money?" Thomas said, shocked.

"We have enough of you Yanks in here that the boss decided to make it easier and just take your currency."

"Good, man. Keep the change, but don't forget this face," Thomas said, placing two quarters on the bar.

The bartender was more than flattered with Thomas's tip. "How could I? You look like a young Humphrey Bogart."

"Fucking love the Limeys," Thomas said to himself as he walked his drinks over to an empty two-top table. Thinking of the benefits his generous tip might get him later that night, he lumsily bumped into a navy seaman, spilling beer all over him.

"Watch where you're fucking going," the tall Navy Boy with a thick upper-class Boston accent said to Thomas.

Thomas was in the wrong and didn't want a bar room brawl on his first leave, so he offered up an apology. "Sorry, buddy, let me buy you a beer to make it up for it." Apparently, military had taught him discipline and when to not act like a moron.

"I'll take you up on that. My name is Ensign Joe Kennedy by the way," he said, reaching out a hand.

"Thomas Whitney, Army Air Force. Sorry again about the spill."

"Occupational hazard," Ensign Kennedy said with a smile.

Thomas ordered Kennedy a beer and once again over-tipped the ever-grateful British bartender.

"Cheers to victory in Europe."

"Cheers to a long and successful post-war life for both of us."

The two sipped their lagers and quickly made light of their volatile introduction. Tyler saw Thomas making a new friend and decided to talk to a few fellow airmen at the bar. They spent enough time together that making new acquaintances in different parts of the bar was far from the worst thing in the world.

"So where are you from, lieutenant?" Kennedy asked.

"San Diego. Where do you hail from?" Thomas asked, knowing the answer would almost certainly be somewhere in New England.

"Boston. My grandfather used to be the mayor there, and my father was actually the ambassador in London for a while. Hopefully, I'll hold office there too someday."

Thomas was unimpressed with Joe's political background, but his hometown did intrigue him. "My wingman is from Massachusetts, and I actually went to prep school there for a year at Deerfield."

"No shit! I was at Choate once upon a time."

"From being school rivals to fighting on the same team, war does some screwy things," Thomas replied.

"My brother Jack graduated from Choate, too—class of 1935. He got shot up bad in the Pacific a few weeks ago on one of those damned PT boats," Joe said in a tone that was so casual you would've thought he was talking about his brother falling off a bike.

"Is he gonna be alright?"

"Jack will be fine. He's already back out there navigating those floating coffins and killing Japs. Probably banged every island girl in the Pacific, too. He's a hall of fame Cocksman."

With each accolade Joe listed about his brother Jack, Thomas grew more and more impressed with this alpha-male that seemed similar to him. "I'd love to meet him."

"After the war, you should come by Hyannis Port to our summer compound. Plenty of beers and broads there for a fellow like you," Joe offered as if he had known Thomas for years.

"My family's originally from Scituate. Is that far from Hyannis Port?" Thomas's knowledge of Massachusetts geography wasn't very accurate.

"Not far, I guess. It's on Cape Cod, and Scituate's about halfway between Boston and Cape Cod."

The conversation eventually moved to a deeper political discussion, as usually happens with alcohol and mixed ideals.

"What do you think about Hitler?" Joe asked somewhat quietly, as not to raise an issue with the many patrons who'd had their lives turned upside down by the actions of the evil Nazi leader.

Thomas had mostly kept his thoughts to himself—sans venting to Tyler—since he got to England, but he had enough beer in him that he stated what was seemingly always on his mind. "Stalin and those commie bastards should be where we're focusing our energy and resources right now. The next war will be bigger and against communism."

"I told my father back in thirty-four that Hitler knew what he was doing and would raise a superior army. When he told Franklin, he got ridiculed and labeled un-American. Now look where we are," Joe said, as every sip of beer brought his accent out more and more.

Thomas looked at the eldest Kennedy, and in a weird way, saw a reflection of himself. Uppity, upper-class upbringing, idealistic about America's position on Nazism and communism, yet still in Europe, ready to fight and die for the principles of democracy. "I saw Stalin's wrath firsthand in 1935. Russia is fucked, and communism is why."

"In the post-war world, people like us will be calling the shots. My Old Man has been grooming me for years. Fuck the commies. Hell, if Uncle Adolf wants to join our side, we'll take him."

Had Thomas had similar thoughts? Absolutely, but the sheer balls it took to say that out loud in England of all places, a country that had been decimated by German carpet bombing for over three years, was impressive. This was a different kind of guy—one that had the weird mix of privileged upbringing, idealism, and courage. "I mean, if Lucifer wanted to come out against communism, we'd take him on our team," Thomas said, spinning a 1941 Winston Churchill quote about likening the devil to Stalin and welcoming the prince of darkness if it meant defeating Hitler to fit his own narrative.

"When I'm President and my brothers, Jack, Teddy, and Bobby, are making policies, communism will be no more," Joe answered, as if being the president of the United States was a job as easy as signing up and showing up.

As someone who had no issue being braggadocious—especially after a few drinks—even Thomas was taken aback with the young man's confidence. Not only was he convinced he was going to be president, but he was going to be the first Irish Catholic President of the United States. The fine line between confidence and fantasy were blurred with Ensign Kennedy, but rather than call him out for his bullshit, it intrigued him more and more. "That sounds like quite the America."

"It'll be grand. Communism will be defeated, poverty will cease to exist, and the American way of life will be the gold standard for the rest of the world."

His "campaign promises" that weren't campaign promises made him sound more and more like a career politician than a twenty-something-year-old flyboy. He had clearly been groomed for this and would tell anyone who would listen, but Thomas liked his style. That being said, it was getting late in the evening, and they were still combatants in a war zone. "It's been fun, but I need to get going. Back on the base tomorrow morning, and probably back in the unfriendly skies not too long after that."

"See you in Hyannis Port the first summer after the war. Teddy, Bobby, and Jack will love you," Joe said, reaching out his hand.

"I look forward to it," Thomas replied, and the Bay Stater vanished into the London night. He began looking around the now-emptying bar for Tyler.

"Who was your new friend?" Tyler asked as the two prepared to leave for the hotel room they had rented for the evening.

"Joe Kennedy, navy boy, from a political family in Massachusetts. Strikes me as a future president of the United States himself."

"His family's pretty well-known in the Bay State," Tyler replied.

"Either way, that was one interesting guy."

"Glad you made a new friend. Any chance he wants to transfer to the Army and become your new cellmate?"

"And deprive you of the honor of my presence? Why would anyone do that?"

"I thought the Geneva Convention banned cruel and unusual punishment by the Army. Let down yet again."

"What do the Swiss know? They don't even have skin in this game!"

Little did Thomas know that Switzerland being on the sidelines while the rest of the world played the most dangerous game of football in human existence would come in handy down the line. Keeping skin out of the game may have been the difference between him staying alive and dying.

***

Switzerland/France Border

October 19, 1943

1500 hours

Switzerland was *the* bastion of neutrality in Europe in World War II, and the Swiss guarded their borders carefully, for good reason. For all the hell that was engulfing Europe, the mountainous country remained mostly untouched, and the Swiss wanted to keep it that way. This made sneaking in across the border a little bit harder than getting into a bar in San Diego underage.

"German troops on one side of the road, Swiss troops on the other. No way we get through that border crossing," Thomas said as he and Rebecca crouched down in bushes on a hill about a hundred yards from neutrality.

"Do you still have your knife?" Rebecca asked.

"Obviously."

"Let's go about half a mile down from the road and the crossing, cut a hole in the fence, and crawl through."

"Roger that. Let's just hope there aren't any patrols on either side when we start slicing."

"We made it across enemy territory with only a few shots fired. It'd be awful for our luck to run out now."

Once the sun went down, the two did just that. Quietly cutting a hole in the border fence, they sprinted as far into Switzerland as they could without arousing any suspicion from the guard posts half a mile apart in either direction.

"Now what?" Thomas asked. He hoped Rebecca would know where they were going now that they were on the other side of the border.

"I don't know how to get to Bern on foot, and we don't have papers or money to take a train or bus."

Thomas just laughed and offered up the best idea he could. "Let's steal a car and follow the road signs."

"I beg your pardon?!"

"I'll get us a car, you translate some road signs, and we're in Bern within the hour. What's wrong with that idea?"

"You want to commit a crime to help us escape?"

"Technically, we're committing a crime even being here. What's one more at this point?"

"You're crazy," she tutted, paused a moment, then sighed, "but I want to stop running and looking over my shoulder. If that means causing someone else's day to be bad, then so be it."

"Done deal. Let's carjack some unlucky son of a bitch."

They found a quiet dirt road and waited for their opportunity.

"When we see a car, stand out in front of it and get the driver to stop. I'll come to his door from the side."

"Sounds like you've done this before," Rebecca said with a bit of a laugh as Thomas *did* sound like a bit of a criminal.

"Nope. Always wanted to be a bad boy, though."

Sure enough, right around sunrise, a Saab with just one passenger slowly drove along their road.

"Now," Thomas said as Rebecca sprinted into the middle of the road to put their plan in action.

The driver slammed on the breaks. Before the driver could put his thoughts together, Thomas was standing at the driver's side door with his pistol aimed right at the man's head, tapping on the window with his free, right hand. The man opened the door with his hands up, and Thomas pressed the pistol to his chest and waved Rebecca over to serve as a translator.

"Tell him this isn't anything personal. I don't want to hurt him, we just need a car."

Rebecca repeated those sentiments in French and waited for Thomas to add his statement. Luckily for them, the driver understood the French instructions. Thomas let go of the man, took his belt off, and put it over the man's eyes as a blindfold.

"Tell him to walk that way," Thomas began as he pointed toward a lightly wooded area, "and wait two minutes. Then he can take the blindfold off, and I promise I won't shoot him."

"What if he walks into a tree?" Rebecca asked.

"Jesus fucking Christ! Just translate and tell him what I said so we can get the fuck out of here."

Rebecca did just that as the man walked into the Swiss woods, and the pair of carjackers sped off into the early morning.

"There's a road sign ahead. Tell me what it says," Thomas said as he slowed down enough for the sign to become legible.

"Bern, twenty-eight kilometers. Stay on this road."

"When we get to Bern, are we just going to drive around, screaming out your sister's name until she finds us?"

"No, I know where she lives. When we get into the city, I can figure it out, provided she still lives there."

"And what if she doesn't?" Thomas asked as he sped toward Bern.

"Then we go to the U.S. Consulate there. If they'll take you back, since I helped save you, maybe they can find room for me, too."

"Deal."

The rest of the car ride was silent as Thomas navigated the Swiss roads with the ease of the Pacific Coast Highway. When the city limits of Zurich were upon them, Rebecca took over as the navigator. She recognized countless landmarks from the many journeys to visit her sister in Bern.

"What am I looking for?" Thomas asked as he drove through street after street that all started to look the same.

"She lives between the Aare River and the U.S. Embassy, almost directly across the river from the Barengraben."

"What the fuck is a Barengraben?" Thomas asked. He wasn't sure if Rebecca had just made up a word to screw with him.

"The bear pit of Bern. It's been a symbol of the city for many years," Rebecca explained.

"Beers you drink, or bears that can maul you to pieces?"

"The animal. They are majestic to look at."

Thomas had seen his share of large beasts during his countless trips to the San Diego Zoo, and he surely wouldn't have minded taking a look at what he assumed was Bern's answer to the zoo, but there wasn't time. He drove parallel to the river and hoped the signs and landmarks would be enough for Rebecca to find her way.

"That's her building right there," Rebecca said as she pointed to a small apartment building on the left side of the road.

Thomas made a sharp left turn across a few lanes of traffic and pulled up right in front of the building that represented Rebecca's freedom. They had been through a lot together, and each owed their respective survival to the other, but this was the end of the line.

"Go in. I'll wait outside for you if she's not there."

"You're not coming inside with me?"

"No, this is about you and your sister. Your family deserves privacy right now."

"Well, thank you for all that you've done."

"I'm sorry about your parents, but I'm glad you're where the Gestapo can't get you."

"I haven't seen my sister in four years, since before the war. I don't know what I'll say or how I'll break the news to her."

Thomas wanted to make a crass joke about shooting straight, but for once in his life, he bit his tongue. "Just speak from the heart and be direct, like you always are. I'll be waiting outside, just in case."

Rebecca cracked a real smile for the first time in an eternity and embraced the airman she had escaped the jaws of death alongside. "Thank you, but I should be going now. The American Embassy is two blocks that way," she pointed northwest and exited the car. She took a deep breath in and headed toward her sister's last-known residence.

Sure enough, within ten seconds of knocking, Ariella—or who Thomas presumed was Ariella—came out, and the sisters shared a tearful embrace. Their parents may have been dragged off to an unknown fate, but the sisters were reunited and safe within the treacherous waters that was occupied Europe. Upon knowing that Rebecca was *safe,* Thomas started driving toward the U.S. Embassy. Now it was his turn to get the hell out.

He spied the American flag outside, abandoned the car, and went inside, where a well-dressed clerk sat behind a desk.

"Good afternoon. May I help you?" the clerk hesitantly greeted as the tattered and bloody Thomas walked on the first American soil since he'd been deployed.

"I'm Lieutenant Thomas Whitney. I got shot down coming back from an escort mission a few days ago," he explained.

"Well, welcome back to American soil. Sorry it's not New York or LA and there isn't a pro ball team or a hot dog vendor around," the clerk said as he reached out his hand.

"It'll do," Thomas remarked, shaking the stranger's hand and smiling.

"Ambassador Harrison isn't here right now, but I do have someone who might be of help to you. Follow me."

Thomas followed the clerk down to a room at the end of a long hallway. "Take a seat in here. He'll be right with you."

"Yes, sir," Thomas answered, having no idea who *he* was or what *he* had in store for him, but it was better than hiding in bushes from enemy patrols.

Within minutes, the door burst open. "Who the hell are you?" an older man said to him in an accent that sounded slightly New England. He may have been thousands of miles away from the forty-eight states, but this man was an American—no question. A younger agent trailed behind him.

"Lieutenant Thomas Whitney, U.S. Army Air Corps," Thomas replied loudly and proudly.

"No shit," the man growled. "How'd you end up here in Bern?"

"Shot down over France a few days ago, dodged some German patrols, and used the help of a friend to get here."

"Let's get you some chow and start going over a frame-by-frame of how you got here and what you saw behind enemy lines. How does a ham and cheese sandwich and a cup of coffee sound to you?"

He wasn't much of a ham and cheese guy but, given his lack of food over the last few days, it sounded pretty damn good. "Like a filet mignon fresh off the grill," he joked.

"I'll have my orderly fetch you just that. We have some work to do. Tell us everything you saw while you were out there."

"Start with any and all intel that will help us win the war," the agent piped in.

"Well, for starters," Thomas began. "The French Resistance wasn't exactly helpful. I'm sure they're doing a great job being a thorn in the Krauts' side, but they didn't help us much."

"Us?" the agent questioned.

"Myself and the Jewish refugee that helped me. I wouldn't be here if it wasn't for her, sir," Thomas said.

"Noted."

"The only engagement we had with German troops, she fired the first round, and for someone who'd never so much as held a gun, she more than held her own."

"Did she share any intel?"

Thomas wasn't sure how to answer that question. Surely, she had given him enough information to keep his ass alive, but with regards to specific information that would help the Allies' war effort, he couldn't think of a damn thing. "Just how to stay alive when the chips are down and you're in over your head."

The OSS operative never once gave him his name, but Thomas proceeded to spend hours going over maps explaining his ordeal. Every tree, every stream, creek, and rock that he could remember, Thomas told the operator in the hopes his harrowing ordeal would help in some small way to end this never-ending war. He also told the OSS about his little carjacking incident, which—though it wasn't the best look for the U.S. Army—was something he would never be put on the record for. He was a hero now; any rule that got bent in the process could be chalked up as a necessary evil.

"Son, you've done a great service to your country. I'm going to send this intel up the chain. Every bit counts."

"Thank you, sir, but what happens to me now?"

"I've got to put a call in, but I believe you'll be going back to England for now. We have a few transport planes that operate undercover and make runs every few days. One leaves tonight, and I'll have you on it. Given your injuries and what you've gone through, we can send you home if you so choose."

"Home?" Thomas asked, very perplexed.

"You served with great courage, honor, and distinction. It would be my honor to call in a favor and arrange for you to finish your duty Stateside. Maybe even at home in California."

"How'd you know I was from California?" Thomas asked, since he never disclosed where he was from to this still-mysterious operative.

"I'm in the information gathering business, lieutenant. I'd be really shitty at my job if I couldn't figure out where a guy like you is from. Let me guess: surfer, maybe played football in high school," he said as he was the definition of hyper-observant

"Played in college, too, sir. USC Trojans," Thomas boasted. He never passed up on the chance to mention his exploits on the field, even in war.

"Once upon a time, I was a flanker at Yale, and that's all you need to know about me," the operative finished as he left the room.

As soon as he left the room, the same clerk that greeted him at the embassy door came back. "Sit tight here for a couple of hours. We'll get you to the airfield tonight when it's time."

For some, the waiting is the hardest part, but not for Lieutenant Whitney. Being allowed to sit indoors and catch up on some rest was like an act of God. Sure enough, a few hours later, he got a tap on the shoulder. "It's go time," said yet another nameless secret operative as he walked Thomas to a small car—not too different from the one he had stolen that morning—and drove off to a small runway.

"I had no idea there was a base in Switzerland that we were running operations out of," Thomas said to the driver as a means of breaking the ice.

"We don't. This base doesn't exist; neither do we. As far as your commanding officers are concerned, this plane left from Italy, and you were smuggled by a fishing boat in the south of France to our lines in Italy. You speak nothing to anyone about what you've seen over here. Make up some bullshit and be done with it."

"Making up bullshit is kind of my specialty."

"Ours, too," the other unnamed OSS operative said with a hint of a smile.

He was loaded into an unmarked transport and told to simply be quiet. All through the flight, Thomas dozed in and out as the plane made its way toward England. His body and mind were exhausted, but sleep didn't exactly come easy.

As he sat in the transport plane, likely flying over the same place he was on the run, Thomas was alone with his thoughts, and toward the end of the flight, they *really* kept him awake. After all the effort it took to bring Thomas overseas, he wasn't keen on just leaving— even though the OSS offer was still on the table. He didn't really want to check out from the war effort, despite the bumps and bruises, but the never-ending sunshine of California was tempting. The conundrum was one he'd never thought he'd have to face.

His future in the war wasn't the only matter of concern in his brain either. He thought about Rebecca. She was safe and reunited with her sister Ariella, but that family would never again be the same without their parents. He thought about Tyler, who gave his own life so he could have a chance at getting home in one piece. He even thought about Anna for a second; like Rebecca, she too was a fatal victim of tyranny. He once again thought about home, the coast of California, and the salt air and tranquility he promised to resign himself to when this was all over. The end was in sight, but the concept of the end was surely a tricky one to fully understand, especially with the war still very much underway and young men like Tyler dying every day in pursuit of victory.

And then, before he knew it, he was back in England.

"Welcome back," Major Leney greeted upon the transport's arrival in the wee hours of the morning. "I'm sorry about your buddy, Tyler. He was one hell of a flyer. I put him in for the Medal of Honor. Hopefully, Ike sees fit to reward it. I put you in for a Distinguished Flying Cross yourself, and because of your wounds, you'll be getting the complimentary Purple Heart courtesy of Uncle Sam, Dwight David Eisenhower, and Franklin Delano Roosevelt."

"Thank you, sir," Thomas said as he wiped the sleep out of his eyes and readied himself for what was sure to be a great bastard of a briefing and lecture.

"I've got good news and bad news. The good news, as you know, is you can return home to lick your wounds and maybe help sell some war bonds. God knows the crowds would love hearing about the pilot that got shot down over enemy skies and avoided capture. That story'll buy more planes and train more pilots. Might even get you laid a time or two. First time for everything," Major Leney teased.

"And the bad news?" Thomas asked, not in the mood to banter.

"We're short flyers. I need all the experienced pilots I can get, especially with the inevitable invasion across the English Channel. After all you went through, I'd never order you to fly so soon, but it'd really be helping me and the war effort out."

This very situation had played out in Thomas's head on the flight back to freedom, but he knew what the answer was. "I'll stay. Let's win the whole fucking thing," he vowed, then sent a grin to his commanding officer. "And just for the record, sir, I don't need to be selling no damn war bonds to get girls. Hell, I might even teach you a thing or two since we're going to be staying together."

"While I appreciate your enthusiasm to turn me into a fellow womanizing heathen, I'll pass on the Thomas Whitney School of Degeneracy," he chuckled, then patted Thomas on the shoulder. "Seriously, though, make sure you finish that beer you left on the table last week." Major Leney handed Thomas a forty-eight-hour pass, a favor for staying on board.

"Thank you, sir," Thomas said as he thought about that ice-cold stout he needed to finish and all that had transpired since he started sipping on it. "I need one more favor to get me to stay sir."

"What's that?" a bewildered Major Leney asked.

"My father got screwed out of a Purple Heart in 1919. Is there any way he can take mine?"

"You don't have to give up yours for your old man. Hell, I'll even use my pull to get him a few extras for lost time if it means you'll stay over here and fly with us. We'll get you a new plane ASAP," Major Leney said.

"Then that works for me," Thomas said as he walked toward the direction of the officer's club.

A voice called out just as he was entering. "There he is, the hero of the skies."

"Lieutenant Benjamin Brady, how goes the battle?" Thomas replied as he embraced his partner in the skies and poker opponent.

"We're both alive, so it can't be too bad."

"I have a present for you," Thomas said as he reached in his holster and pulled out the lucky revolver.

"I thought I had to win it back?"

"This damn thing kept me alive over there, so as a token of my appreciation for being alive, here it is back."

"I figured you'd want to keep it."

"Got me through hell once. Next time around, I'll get a rabbit's foot or a four-leaf clover, maybe shove a horseshoe up my ass. Change things up a bit," Thomas said, then pulled out his Luger from his jacket. "Besides, I stumbled across this beauty in my travels, and she more than fills the void."

"You son of a bitch! Like everyone has ever said about you, Whitney, you roll in shit and come out smelling like a damned rose."

A bittersweet smile flickered across his face as he thought about the last person to echo those words to him—Tyler, on the day before the fateful mission happened.

"I try," was all he could come up with.

"Glad you're back among the living. Enjoy the beer you're owed," Brady said as he walked away.

"I sure as hell will. See you back in the sky sometime soon."

Before he could go to the bar, Thomas needed to shower. He had the stench of occupied Europe scrubbed off him while he was in Switzerland, but he needed one more to feel like the hell he witnessed was washed off.

He stood in the scalding hot shower and wept. Through everything, he'd kept it together and never let anyone see him dip his head in shame, but it had all hit him at once. Tyler's death, Rebecca's family, the two men they killed. If the flight from Switzerland had given him the chance to make sense of what had happened and what was happening, this shower was proving there was no sense to be made of it. All he could do was carry out the orders he had been assigned and hope to God that somehow, some way, he'd not only get home alive, but the suffering around the globe would end.

He composed himself as he put his uniform back on and prepared to go back out to face reality. For someone who grew up with so much and had put together quite the resume of lifetime accomplishments, accepting helplessness didn't come easy, but if accepting helplessness kept his sanity intact, then that was a trade he'd have to make.

"Time for that damn drink," he said as he walked toward the officer's club and put on a somewhat happy face.

As he sat down on the same barstool he was in when he got the word to go on that fateful mission, he thought once again about that promise he made himself.

"Well, I guess the calamity and that house with an ocean view can wait," Thomas said to himself with a chuckle. His war wasn't over, but because of his efforts and the efforts of millions of other good young men, victory was closer than ever before.

"Deliver us from evil," he said to himself as he sipped that cheap British stout and thought back fondly of Lieutenant Donovan and hoped Rebecca had found the peace and safety she had so longed for. He thought of their faith, hope, and struggles.

He lifted his glass up. "Cheers."

Made in the USA
Middletown, DE
24 December 2020

27910311R00078